IV.

C000019173

A few people I want to thank for their part in helping me finish this
second book in the DI Johnson series.
Thank you to Tara Ford, fellow author and Burnley lass, for your
expertise and guidance.
Thank you to my mum and Alan (surrogate dad) for your
encouragement and belief that I could actually achieve my goal.
At last, but definitely not least,
thank you to my beautiful children,
Ben, Sam, Holly and Georgia,
and not forgetting,
my two grandchildren Isaac and Zara.
We never had much materially as you grew up, but we've always
had love, which no man can put a price on.
We've had more than our fair share of tragedy and cruel twists of
fate, but these are all grist to the mill.

Through trials, we learn,
Through pain we grow,
Through experience, we develop understanding,
Through tears, we gain empathy,
And after everything, we're still standing!

My dream is to build a legacy for you,
because, as corny as it sounds,
you are my everything.

xxx

Mortification

"For it has been granted unto you, on behalf of Christ, not only to believe in Him, but also to suffer for Him"
  Philippians 1, 29 (NIV)

Mortification :- Self-mortification is when a person punishes himself, often physically. Most self-mortification is practiced by deeply religious people.In Christianity, self-mortification is called "mortification of the flesh," and it ranges from self-denial — like not drinking alcohol or fasting — to hitting one's own shoulders and back with a whip or strap. Self-mortification isn't practiced by all Christians, and it is a part of other religions as well, especially for very strict followers. The root word is mortificationem, "a killing, or a putting to death" in Latin — in other words, the killing of a person's desires through self-discipline. (vocabulary.com)

Chapter One. The Warehouse.

It was another busy day at the warehouse. They carried stock for an online store that had rocketed in popularity and sales into a major fashion supplier.

Mohammed was filling his sixth order of the day. The others called him a 'pocket rocket' as he wasn't very tall, but he was fast. He quite liked the nickname as he was proud of his reputation as a good worker. With a 'can do' attitude and an easy going, friendly nature, Mohammed had been made manager of their department around six months ago. His workmates respected his authority as they knew he worked at least as hard, if not harder than they did.

Janet was on her fifth order. She packed the items of clothing into the box with the order printout and sealed it with the tape gun before adding the self adhesive label.

On to the next one, she thought to herself and began scanning the shelves for the next item number.

Janet had worked at the warehouse for just over five months now. She had seen others come and go in that time. It was hard work and only those who were quick and accurate survived more than a couple of months. Janet needed this job. She had three mouths to feed; her own, her three year old son, Harry, and her two year old daughter, Amy. A lot of responsibility for a twenty five year old. She didn't begrudge it one bit though. Those two children were her life. It was a good job too as their two-timing snake of a father was long gone. She was mother, father and provider all rolled into one, but she was more than up to the challenge.

Her dyed, silver grey hair was swept up into a messy bun, but she still wiped the sweat off her forehead with the back of her hand as she worked. Her fitbit said she had already walked well over four thousand steps and it was barely ten o'clock. One thing about this job, it kept you fit, she thought wryly to herself.

Liam worked alongside Janet, picking out his own items to pack. He worked steadily and methodically through his lists and very rarely made mistakes. Liam was tall, wiry and strong. Janet often joked that he was like a machine, like the terminator in the movies, but he merely replied, "I do what I'm paid to do, is all," in his eastern european accent. Janet couldn't quite work him out. He was in his mid twenties too, she guessed, but he came across as much older. He looked, Janet searched for the word, tortured. That was it, tortured, like he had the weight of the world on his shoulders.

Tariq had worked there a little over two weeks now and was just beginning to find his pace as he searched the complicated rack system looking for item numbers. Janet helped him out sometimes when he struggled to find the right shelves. This was Tariq's first job since leaving college, and it was a steep learning curve but he was determined to do it well. The eighteen year old was a quick learner and Janet felt he would make a good picker and packer given time.

"Oi, oi sexy," a voice called over in Janet's direction, breaking her train of thought. It was Darren, grinning broadly as he brought in the next set of orders and began work on the first one. He barely glanced at Liam.

Janet rolled her eyes but grinned back as she took her orders from his outstretched hand. Darren might be a bit on the cheeky side, but she thought he was funny and a man who can make a woman laugh would always seem more attractive, and she did indeed find him very attractive.

Darren was a healthy five foot eleven, with a red beard to match his hair. He tended to wear a similar uniform daily of black t-shirts with heavy metal bandnames on them and black jeans. In his ears were holes around half an inch diameter with black, flesh tunnel rings and around his neck he wore a chunky silver chain. He worked quickly. Despite spending time chatting and laughing his way through the day, he was one of their fastest pickers.

The hours passed by and soon it was five o'clock, another day's work done, home time.

At the end of the shift he hung around, waiting for Janet to get her things. Liam passed him and they said their goodbyes.

Darren coughed as she appeared, zipping up her shoulder bag.

"Would you like a lift home?" he asked her hesitantly.

"You sure?" asked Janet, "That would be great."

Darren nodded his head and smiled. He drove an old mitsubishi colt, with plenty of rust bubbling through the silver paintwork which meant it was probably one MOT away from the scrapyard.

He threw an empty takeaway container over the back seat to clear the way for Janet to sit beside him. As Darren started up the engine, the dvd player started playing Black Sabbaths, Lord of this World. They found conversation easy throughout the journey to Janet's house and were both a little sorry when it ended.

Janet thanked Darren as she climbed out of the little car and he gave a salute in response.

"See you tomorrow sexy," he called before driving away and leaving Janet smiling on the pavement.

Chapter Two. Liam.

Heavy, grey clouds, threatening rain, were being pushed across the leaden sky by a strong, north wind. Liam was glad when he finally arrived home.

Taking off his shoes and socks, he sat down heavily in his favourite chair. It had been a long day. He took out a cigarette, tapped it twice on its packet and put it between his lips. Frowning as he lit it with a green disposable lighter, Liam took a deep, satisfying drag, the orange tip glowed brightly in the growing, late afternoon gloom of the small living room. His head fell back against the back of the chair as he exhaled, his eyes closing as he savoured the taste of the smoke on his tongue and the nicotine in his lungs.

Liam was tired. No, not tired. Liam was exhausted. He had finished a seven 'til five shift and his whole body seemed to cry out for rest. Ten hours of picking out items and packing them into parcels for delivery. Today, however, was a good day as he didn't have to go back out to his second job delivering pizza, which he did three days a week, although the free pizza was a good perk of the job.

Smoke escaped his mouth in a thin stream after a second drag on his cigarette and his shoulders visibly lowered as he began to unwind.

The room was darkening rapidly as twilight fell. The moss green, velour curtains were still open and sprigs of juniper sat in a delicate, cut glass bud vase on the window sill. A small tv sat on a mahogany table in the corner of the room. Liam preferred to read or use his tablet for movies so he didn't see the need of replacing it with a larger one. His mother, Bojana, rarely watched it. The cataracts in her eyes meant she couldn't see well enough to enjoy it.

Green floral wallpaper covered the walls and a deep pile, sage green carpet felt comfortingly soft under his bare feet.

Stubbing out his cigarette, Liam stood and went into the small kitchen to find food. He flicked the light switch and blinked at the harsh glare from the fluorescent tube light.

In the fridge, he found a bowl of grah, a traditional, Slavic bean and meat stew, and put it in the microwave to reheat. His mother, Bojana, usually left him plastic containers filled with food from his childhood she had prepared for him. Other days he would make do with bread and cheese or spicy sausage.

Bojana would be asleep by now in the second bedroom. She lived by the old maxim, early to bed, early to rise.

As the microwave pinged, Liam buttered a thick slice of bread. Placing the bread, and the hot stew, onto a tray along with a glass of milk, he carried them into the living room. Closing the curtains and switching on the overhead light, he then sat down to eat.

After his meal, he lit another cigarette and his mind drifted back to life in the old country. The hills covered with snow and rough tracks with large puddles frozen solid into thick ice. He remembered his fingers being so cold he could hardly open the door to their little house on the hill. His toes swollen and purple with painful chilblains from the long walks in cold winters.

Liam recalled the streams and rivers flowing with icy water that bisected the villages. One side of the river for the living, and the other side for the dead. He remembered the curious thin bridges for the dead to cross over the river to the netherworld and the red string tied to branches that was part of the ancient Vlach magic.

The magic had scared him as a child. He'd been brought up in an Orthodox Christian household after his Vlach mother married his Orthodox father, Drago. His father had been killed in the war over two decades ago, when Yugoslavia still featured on maps. Drago was taken out with the other men from their village and shot, despite his grandmother's spell to keep him from harm. Liam was lucky not to have been killed himself and only his young age saved him. His grandmother, Dobrilka, gave him, in her words, 'powerful, magic water' with herbs and coal at the bottom to drink which tasted strange. She told him not to complain as in times long past, the spell was made using the 'ghastly' water, that is water saved from the washing of the deceased. Dobrilka had laughed her cackling laugh with thin lips and toothless gums at the expression of horror and disgust on Liam's young face as he listened.

He despised the old Vlach magic. To him, it was primitive and dangerous.

The past still haunted Liam. They were dark times full of fear and uncertainty. Long days and even longer nights of sadness, terror and tears.

He remembered the long march, when the women and young children were forced from their village, over the mountains to a safer land, away from the violence and hatred. Babies cried and wailed for days, before they fell forever silent. Too frail and small to survive the nights out in the open, in sub zero temperatures. Grandmother Dobrilka had died during the march. She was simply too old and tired to make the journey. They had tried to dig a grave in the frozen ground with their hands and sticks but it was impossible. In the end, with torn and bloody nails from the frozen ground, they simply left her, by the side of the road, covered with a few branches from the black pine trees that grew there.

Sometimes he felt his difficult childhood had affected his mind, but he tried to push away such unwanted thoughts. He had to remind himself that he was safe now. Sometimes he would pray, "Spasi me od pameti," which translates as, "Save me from my mind."

Stubbing out his cigarette, Liam stood and took his tray into the kitchen and quickly washed the dishes before going to bed to read his bible.

Chapter Three. Having a fag.

"Room for a little 'un?" said Cheryl squeezing herself in the middle of Liam and Darren, lighting her menthol cigarette with a pink lighter.

She stood, hunched over, shielding the flame with her hand from the cold wind that blew noisily through the smoking shelter.

She inhaled deeply, fuschia pink lips drawing air through the cigarette to make sure it was properly lit before pocketing the lighter and standing more upright. She let the first lung full of smoke out with a satisfied sigh.

"It's bloody freezing lads! It's a good job I've got two handsome fellas to keep me warm, eh?" said Cheryl, winking at Liam.

Liam smiled with more than a touch of embarrassment, she must be what, twenty years older than him?

Her constant flirty comments and her 'accidental' brushing against him made him cringe, but he put up with it because he felt a little sorry for her and her desperate attempts to attract male attention. Liam thought that, at her age, late forties, she was probably scared of ending up alone.

"They could' ve made a better job of this shelter," complained Cheryl , "It blows a gale here and it creaks so much I think the roofs going to blow off the top one day!"

Darren laughed, "Reckon it's so we don't get too comfy and stay out too long?"

"You might 'ave something there Darren," Cheryl replied, "I wouldn't put it past this lot."

Liam sucked hard on the last of his filterless cigarette, before dropping it on the floor and grinding it to tobaccoey shreds with his booted foot.

"Well, back to work, see you later, Cheryl, Darren," he said in his thick croatian accent, nodding a goodbye to each as he spoke their names.

"Bye Liam," Cheryl answered, blatantly watching his bum as he walked back into the warehouse.

Then, turning to Darren she said pointedly, "He's a nice looking fella, that one. Bit of a strong, silent type. Just how I like 'em."

Darren laughed along kindly with Cheryl, as he smoked his cigarette.

"He is single, isn't he?" asked Cheryl hopefully.

Darren nodded,
"He still lives with his mum I think."
Cheryl smiled, "You'll have to let him know I'm single too,"
Darren lightheartedly said, "I think he might know Cheryl."
"Well, sometimes they need a bit of a push," she responded, "You make sure you tell him."
"Ok," agreed Darren, "I'll tell him."
It was getting cold outside, shame they weren't allowed a fag inside, thought Darren. Cheryl must be freezing in that thin blouse. He stifled a laugh when he noticed her nipples under the material, poking out like a pair of chapel hat pegs, as his dad used to say. Yep, I guess she is cold, he thought, feeling amused.
"How's your little dog getting on?" asked Darren, trying to make conversation, and keep his eyes focused above her neck.
"Aww, Poppet," smiled Cheryl, warming to the theme, "He's just as gorgeous as ever. You'll have to come over and visit us. His fur! You wouldn't believe how silky soft it is, and if you hold him, you can feel his little heart racing ten to the dozen. He's good company he is, with me being on my own, like."
Darren nodded, he also lived alone, but was young enough to enjoy the freedom and novelty of solitude.
"Good to hear he's doing well, he's a cute little thing," said Darren.
Cheryl had a photo of Poppet in a silver frame engraved with paw prints in her desk. Poppet, the black and white Pomeranian, was loved and cherished by Cheryl. When at home, in her little bungalow, she spoke to him as if he were a little human and he was absolutely spoiled rotten.
"Who's mummy's good little boy? Yes you Poppet, you are. You are, yes you are," she would say, speaking in a voice an octave higher than usual.
Poppet gave her an excuse to go out for a walk in the fresh air and she found him useful as a conversation starter when she came across attractive male dog walkers.
Darren stubbed out his cigarette on one of the sturdy wooden posts that held up the sloping, corrugated roof of the makeshift shelter.

"Give Poppet a hug from me,Cheryl" said Darren cheerily, before heading back into the warehouse.

"Will do!" she answered with a raise of her hand. She should have put her coat on, thought Cheryl as she stood quietly smoking, alone, shivering from the distinct chill in the air. Summer had definitely been and gone, she thought to herself, downhill from here.

Putting out her cigarette, Cheryl hurried back into the warmth of her office. Uttering a determined, "Right," and settling herself back down in her ergonomically designed, and very comfortable, office chair, she tapped her shocking pink nails on the computer keyboard, brought up the payroll programme and got back to work, filling in the timesheets.

Chapter Four. Mohammed.

Mohammed felt weak. He had the beginnings of a bad cold and was feeling its effects. It was now two o'clock in the afternoon and he was counting down the hours until his shift finished at five.

Janet and Darren were joking away with each other as usual. You could cut the sexual tension between them with a knife he thought to himself smiling. He wished they'd just hurry up and get together. Young love eh? Everyone can see it but them. Too busy trying to be cool so neither makes the first move.

He chuckled to himself as he worked. He remembered when he first met his wife, Nasreen. He was just the same. Little sideways glances and smiles but too nervous to speak. Luckily his parents had also noticed Nasreen. She was a young woman they approved of as a match, so they had done most of the legwork for him.

That was almost nineteen years ago now. They'd had a good marriage, most definitely a love match.

"Come on Tariq, them boxes aren't gunna pack 'emselves, mate," he called across the warehouse floor.

Caught day-dreaming, the eighteen year old jumped at the sound of his name and resumed packing. Mohammed smiled, Tariq was doing well, but the young often needed a nudge until they built up their stamina for a full day's work.

Liam was methodically working his way through his orders. Mohammed had never had cause to give him a nudge. He knew Janet called him 'the Terminator' partly because of his strong accent, but mainly because of his way of working. Steady and focused, always so serious, almost robotic thought Mohammed. He was definitely a good worker, an asset to the factory.

Taking his break, he made his way to the staff room. Mohammed's head felt as though it were stuffed with cotton wool. Time for another Lemsip, he said to himself. He boiled the kettle and made the hot lemon, cold remedy. Sitting at a table by himself, he slowly sipped the scalding drink, it felt soothing on his scratchy throat. It was the time of year when everyone started to get colds and other viruses. The summer warmth had gone and the colder air of autumn had arrived. The warehouse was a big area with high ceilings, impossible to heat properly, so it was always cold. If the worker's immune systems weren't tip top, viruses were ready to attack. Then people were off sick and productivity went down.

Mohammed would bring string bags of oranges in for his team, out of his own pocket, for vitamin C, to keep them healthy.

Unfortunately, it hadn't appeared to work on his own immune system, as he now had this beggar of a cold.

Nasreen would put extra chili in his dinner tonight to help sweat it out of him.

The lemsip was beginning to take effect, the shivers were less and his head felt clearer. Time to get back to work on the warehouse floor.

"Come on Tariq, get a wriggle on," he called out as he crossed the concrete floor.

Darren and Janet looked deep in conversation too.

"Hey you two, stop chatting and get packing!"

"Yes Boss!" said Darren laughing. He'd finally asked Janet out on a date, and she had said yes. He cheerfully got back to work, whistling away to himself happily.

Janet smiled to herself as she continued to pick and pack, feeling the butterflies of excitement in her tummy.

Mohammed pushed himself to get to the end of the working day, looking frequently at his watch, disappointed that the hands moved round so slowly.

Walking to the office for more orders, he coughed and sniffed.

"You don't look well Mo," said a concerned looking Cheryl, quickly rising from her chair and walking around the desk. She put her hand on his forehead, it felt hot.

"I think you've got a temperature, lovely," she said worriedly, "You should be at home, tucked up in bed with a good woman!"

Mohammed laughed at the jokey comment.

"I'm fine. Not long to go, then home to rest," he replied.

Cheryl looked at the wall clock, forty minutes to go. Hardly worth him going home now.

"Ok, if you're sure, but if you get any worse…"

"Then I'll let you know," finished Mohammed with a weak smile, "Forty minutes and it's the weekend!"

He collected another batch of orders, taking them back through to the warehouse, feeling Cheryl's eyes on his back as he went.

Those last forty minutes dragged, but it was finally home time.

Mohammed went to get his coat and lunchbox from the staff room. Darren and Janet were already in there, Darren had started giving Janet a lift home each night.

Liam and Tariq were already out the door and on their way home. Mohammed, Janet and Darren walked out together and said their goodbyes in the car park.

Darren and Janet, talking animatedly, walked to Darren's beat up Mitsubishi colt.

Mohammed watched them together as he fastened his seatbelt. He smiled. Those two were made for each other, he thought as he started the car and made his way home, glad the working week was over.

Chapter Five. The Library.

It was Saturday. Liam allowed himself a lie in until eight on Saturdays and then he was up, showered, shaved, dressed and out of the door by eight thirty to walk to the library in the centre of town. The air was fresh in his lungs with a slight nip in the air.
A beautiful September day.
The roads were fairly quiet this early on the weekend and he enjoyed the excercise. He walked down Colne road, passing the prairie fields where football was already being played on the all weather pitch. Then past semi detached and detached houses with long front gardens separating their inhabitants from the noise of the road. Trees grew at regular intervals out of the black tarmac pavements providing homes for grey squirrels, who occasionally scampered over the path.
The sun was bright but it was too late in the year for it to be overly warm. Further along, and the houses were built smaller, in stone terraces with tiny forecourts, just big enough for a couple of rose bushes. No trees grew from the pavements here, only crisp packets, takeaway containers and the odd needle discarded by a junkie.
Liam walked on, almost there now, the traffic was getting heavier and the first customers were beginning to park by the Sainsbury supermarket. Crossing the road, the path led into the very heart of the town and Liam followed its descent and continued onwards to his destination, the towns central library.
Climbing up the familiar, sandstone steps, he admired the grandeur of the building. It stood, solid and imposing, like some stately

mausoleum or ziggurat temple to literature. It had been built in the late nineteen twenties when classical styling was back in vogue and buildings were designed to impress. At the top of the wide steps, two fluted, Doric columns stood sentry either side of the old, wooden and glass doors. On entering the library, the smell of beeswax polish and musty books hung in the air giving a sense of solemnity that demanded hushed tones and reverence within its walls. Edwardian tiles and stained glass skylights added to the church-like ambience of the building and Liam felt the weight of its history and grandiosity.

He climbed the the staircase to the reference library, holding the banister rail worn smooth by thousands of hands through time. He was here to find knowledge. To research. To delve into the shadows of the past, the ancestry of families. To explore their history and connections. He sat at one of the public computers and began his work. He did this every Saturday. Recording his findings as he worked and then printing them out to add to his files.

Today was Sunday. An early snowfall had given Pendle hill an icing sugar dusting. Deceptively pretty, only the hardiest would climb her today. The scree would move underfoot and the stony out crops would fool the less experienced as the glass-like, black ice lay as an invisible, treacherous layer upon them. Liam, however, would climb this hill, every morning except for the sabbath, which for him was each Saturday,
whether rain or shine, sunbaked or frozen, he would climb her. It was his routine, his personal challenge and he would no more omit his daily climb than he would omit waking each morning. His self discipline was uncompromising.

The sun was barely peeping over the horizon and Liam was climbing. The lavender hues were giving way to pale lemon as the sun crept slowly upwards.

His breathing was laboured, his lungs burned, he tasted the bitter taste at the back of his throat and clouds of vapour constantly left his mouth, but his pace remained steady. Feeling the pain of the sharp gravel he placed inside his boots before every climb spurred him onwards.

He needed the pain. He needed to feel. He needed to suffer.

He was almost at the summit, he saw the circle of laid stones surrounding the upright stone trig point. Once at the top, he paused to catch his breath. He turned his face to the east just in time to see the rising sun gild the clouds, then set them aflame with oranges and reds.

Nature has such a raw, awe inspiring beauty thought Liam gazing at the vivid hues colouring the eastern sky with wonder and respect.

The watery sun continued its ascent and the colours paled as Liam began his walk back down the hill.

After riding his motorcycle home, Liam showered, dressed and ate a simple breakfast with his mother Bojana. Then they would spend the rest of the morning at church.

In the afternoon, after their lunch, they'd spend the time cleaning the flat together and getting the week's washing done.

The Horvats were creatures of habit, and the familiar routine meant the mundane jobs got done. They liked it that way, it had served them well for years.

Chapter Six. Barrowford.

Elsewhere in the town, Ian Johnson sat drinking his coffee from a large white, bowl shaped cup as he watched the goldfinches and sparrows visiting the bird table in his garden. Orange-red rudbeckias and the firey stems of cornus stood out in sharp contrast to the green backdrop of shiny leaved laurels. Heavy apricot flowers still bloomed on the climbing rose planted by the patio and the last of the nasturtiums scrambled across the borders with their vivid orange and yellow trumpets. Ian loved nature and plants. He found gardening therapeutic and destressing. Almost an antidote to the poison of human depravity he often found in his work as a Detective Inspector leading investigations into heinous crimes including murder.

Eve sat opposite him sipping her tea from a tall, gold patterned mug. Her hair was a vivid, firey red and hung, wild and long framing her porcelain pale face. A deep, bottle green polish covered her long nails and a solitary silver ring with a large, oval carnelian stone adorned her slim fingers.

This morning, Eve wore a silk kimono style dressing gown in rusts and greens. She looked out of the french doors at their secluded garden. It was such a charming outlook that seemed to change almost daily with the seasons and the weather. A magpie landed on the grass, sending the smaller birds fluttering away. Another joined the first magpie. 'Two for joy,' thought Eve and smiled to herself. The black and white birds marched proudly around inspecting the lawn for worms before disappearing noisily into the trees, leaving the way clear again for their smaller cousins.

Eve and Ian had been together for most of their lives and neither could imagine a future without the other.

Eve was the perfect complement to his character. The perfect antithesis to the serious, dour and depressing nature of a lot of Ian's workload, she filled their home with creativity and light. Eve painted beautiful, vibrant works of art full of life and energy in the time she wasn't teaching art at the local college. They'd never had children of their own, but had brought up an adopted brother and sister, for whom they'd provided stability, love and security. The children were both grown now and living happy, independent lives of their own. Yasmin was living in Hebden Bridge with her girlfriend Rose, and worked as a psychologist in Manchester. Joel technically still lived at home, but spent every weekend at his girlfriend, Molly's flat in town. He was fully qualified now and making a real go of his fledgling plumbing business.

"We should go out for lunch," Eve suggested suddenly, "Make the most of the sunshine."

Ian smiled and nodded in agreement.

"I've got a couple of pieces to drop off to the gift shop at the Barrowford Heritage Centre gift shop. Why don't we have lunch at that nice, little cafe there?" Eve continued.

"Perfect!" replied her husband squeezing her hand.

They sipped their drinks in the leisurely way reserved for weekend breakfasts. Comfortable in the silence as they savoured the peace. An hour or so later, they were in Ian's dark green Astra, heading down the motorway to Barrowford. Turning off by Nelson and Colne college they drove down Barrowford's main street before turning right and into the car park of the heritage centre. Eve opened the car boot and took out two paintings, each about two foot square. One depicted a view of Pendle Hill set against a vibrant sunset. The other was a study of an apricot coloured rose from their garden, standing in a green, glass vase. She carried them carefully into the gift shop.

"Hello again Eve," said a cheery voice from behind the counter, "Brought us more goodies?"

"Hi Anne," Eve replied, "Yes, two more. The prices are on them already."

"Fab, I'll get them out on display," said Anne, casting an approving eye over the two paintings.

Eve was looking at some jewellery. She selected a pair of dangly silver earrings with peridots, blue apatite and black onyx set into a peacock feather design.

Impulsively, she bought them and immediately put them in her ears. Leaving the shop, they strolled around the walled garden. Ian picking off an odd herb leaf, crushing it between his fingers and inhaling the scents of its released oils. Spearmint, zingy and uplifting. Sage, fresh and purifying. Lavender, heady and relaxing. They made their way leisurely around the museum, reading the labels explaining the exhibits.

'The Pendle Witch Trials, 1612, at the assizes at Lancaster, twenty persons were tried.'

A copy of an engraving told of the trials where the unlucky inhabitants of nearby towns were tried, convicted and hanged for the crime of witchcraft. Their names were listed. Old and young, all had been forced to confess to all kinds of magic and devilry. They spoke of familiars in the guise of animals that visited them to drink their blood, and effigies of clay that they stuck pins and thorns in to cause ailments.

"What horrible times to live in" said Eve, "It just took one accusation and your death warrant was signed."

Ian nodded, "And there are countries where that can still happen. I've seen it on the internet. Old women accused by villagers and burned to death."

"Terrible!" exclaimed Eve, shaking her head.

"I think that's enough of the dark side for one day, let's go eat," suggested Ian, changing the subject.

"I like your thinking," replied his wife laughing, "I'm actually pretty hungry!"

They chose a table by the window in the courtyard cafe and passed the rest of the afternoon eating jacket potatoes and salad and then chatting over coffee and excellent homemade cake.

Chapter Seven. Eve.

Eve Johnson stood in the converted loft that she used as a studio. A bank of velux windows made the space light and airy. A large, canvas stood on the easel and Eve was sketching her preliminary design. The tip of her pencil made a scratching sound as she worked making sweeping lines on the textured surface.

She was drawing a peacock. She loved the jewel tones of the bird's feathers and wanted to capture their vibrancy in a painting. After sketching, she loaded her palette with ultramarine, cerulean blue, titanium white, viridian green, sap green, burnt umber and yellow ochre and began to paint.

They'd lived in the large, Edwardian house for over two decades now. Eve had fallen in love with the place as soon as she'd seen the light pouring through the original stained glass panels surrounding the old front door casting pools of jewel coloured light on the parquet floor.

Eve and her husband Ian, now Detective Inspector Johnson, had brought up two children within its walls and the place was their forever home, full of happy memories.

Using long, curved strokes of the brush, she began to build up the body of the bird using various shades of greens and blues.

Painting was both Eve's passion and profession. She also tutored part-time at the local college. After the initial financial struggle of their relationship, Ian and Eve were now comfortably well off.

Property prices had always been low in Burnley. The initial buying price of their home was sixty seven thousand. It had seemed an enormous amount at the time they signed their mortgage deal, but as the years passed, and prices rose it seemed more and more affordable. They had been mortgage free for over a year now, they had modest savings and they had everything they needed in life. Life was good.

Eve painted. Totally absorbed in her art and the creative process, lunchtime came and went unnoticed. Eventually, she lost the light, as thick, grey clouds began to fill the sky and Eve was forced to call time on her painting.

Cleaning her brushes, Eve suddenly realised she was thirsty and when she had dried the brushes, went downstairs to the large kitchen to make herself a green tea in her favourite china mug.

Chapter Eight. Hebden Bridge.

Yasmin couldn't remember much about life before Ian and Eve. To her, they were as much a mum and dad as any natural parent could be. They'd welcomed her and Joel into their home with open arms. What she could remember, were the emotions. When she first arrived, she felt constantly on watch for signs of danger, fearful and suspicious of everything. It wasn't long before she began, for possibly the first time in her young life, to feel safe, although she did try her best to test Ian and Eve to see if they could be totally trusted. They passed every test with love and understanding and gradually, Yasmine began to believe they were a permanent fixture in her and her little brother's lives. Now, due to the love and protection her adoptive parent's had provided, Yasmin was no longer a little, scared girl but a strong, confident and well balanced young woman, comfortable in her own skin.

Yasmin and Rose lived in a small, stone built terraced cottage set on a steep hill in the small market town of Hebden Bridge. Fabulous in the summer, but a little perilous in the freezing Yorkshire winters. Thankfully, the gritting lorries were quick off the mark at the first signs of ice or snow.

Hebden bridge was a very traditional, even quaint, little place, with lots of old cobbles and a quirky arched bridge over the river Hebden; the Hebden Bridge. Once a stop on the packhorse route supplying cotton mills, now it was a trendy, sought after location for young professionals who had a taste for country living but with the comforts of the city not too far away.

Rose was everything Yas could have hoped for in a partner. Beautiful, with hair the same colour as her name, a soft rose-pink, a loving nature and a good cook. What more could a girl ask for!

They both loved the pretty, little town with lots of small, independent shops, pubs and cafés. They had visited frequently when they were both at Leeds University, enjoying the easy going, avant guarde, LGTB friendly, ambience. They'd taken a narrow boat ride on the canal that ran through the town, they'd strolled, hand in hand, around the craft stalls and stopped for drinks in the quirky, local pubs. They fell completely in love with the higgeldy piggeldy character of the town and decided they would make it their home after graduating.

After weeks of searching, they'd found a cosy, two bedroomed cottage up for rent.

They'd lived there happily for the past year now. Hebden Bridge was known as the 'lesbian capital of the UK,' so it seemed a natural step for them to move there among like-minded people. They'd made friends easily and felt very much at home.

Yasmin commuted daily to Manchester to work as a psychologist in the children's hospital, a job she absolutely loved.

Rose had studied philosophy with a special interest in paganism and now rented a small shop in the town selling herbal teas alongside spells and incantations. She also sold pagan paraphernalia in an online version of her shop called, unsurprisingly, 'Pagan Paraphernalia.'

Life was good for the couple who shared their lives with two jet-black cats, Elemanzer or 'Ellie' for short, and Akuba.

Akuba was named after the Japanese word for 'witch,' whilst Elemanzer was named after a witches familiar spoken about by Mathew Hopkins, a successful witch finder in the mid sixteen hundreds.

Both cats were well loved and well fed.

They were allowed almost the full run of the little house, including their owners bed. The only exception being the spare bedroom which Rose used as her office and overflow stockroom, so needed to remain cat-hair free.

After a full day's work, the little family lit their cosy woodburning stove and snuggled on the sofa to eat wholesome, home cooked, vegetarian dishes.

Todays meal was sweet potato and chick pea curry served with rice. "This is sooo good Rose," said Yasmin appreciatively, as she used a chapati to mop up some of the spicy sauce.

"Ta, it's not bad is it," Rose replied, "What time are we going over to your dads for his birthday?"

Yasmin swallowed her mouthful before answering, "Around three, and mum's cooking for us. My brother Joel and his girlfriend, Molly will be there too. Should be fun."

Rose nodded, "Am looking forward to it. I like your family. Have you bought a present?"

"I ordered a bottle of good scotch and I found a gorgeous green decanter to put it in at the antiques fair at Mytholmroyd," said Yasmin, "He's going to love it."

Rose smiled lovingly at Yasmin. She felt so lucky to have found her, with her pretty face, caring nature and intelligence.

As Rose had cooked, Yasmin washed up the pots and pans before they cosied up together on the squishy blue sofa to watch tv together with the two cats curled up on their laps. Life was most definitely good.

Chapter Nine. Going out, out.

Darren had finally asked her out!

Janet was carefully applying her make-up. Choosing a deep burgundy shade, she brushed it across her lids and socket line to create a smoky eye effect. She outlined her eyes with black pencil and then brushed mascara through the lashes. She smiled at her reflection in the dressing table mirror as she thought of Darren and their coming date. Brushing blusher onto the apples of her cheeks she wondered where they would be going. He had told her it was a surprise. Knowing he was into old school metal music, she wondered if he would be taking her to watch a band or something. She finished her look by choosing lipstick in a matte burgundy shade. It had been quite a while since she'd last been on a date, and she was feeling a little nervous, so wanted to look her best. After her makeup, Janet began straightening her dyed silver grey hair. She took small sections and slowly ran the straighteners down each one to give her hair a silky smooth finish.

Standing, she looked in the full length mirror and pulled straight the hem of her black cotton shirt. Turning to the left, Janet checked the curve of her backside in her jeans, always worried it was too big. She pulled on her black, suede boots and picked up her bag.

Downstairs, her grandmother sat on the small, tan coloured sofa, crocheting. As Janet entered the room, her grandma put down the crochet work and exclaimed, "Ah, you look lovely Janet, so you do!" in her Irish accent, still strong after decades of living in Burnley.

Janet smiled at the complement. The doorbell rang.

"Off you go then," grandma said, "You go enjoy yourself."

Janet thanked her grandma, kissed her cheek, grabbed her leather jacket and went outside where a smiling Darren waited.

"Oi Oi Gorgeous," Darren said and clicked his tongue, "Looking good!"

Janet smiled and Darren opened the taxi door for her to get in.

The night was dark and moonless as they drove through quiet streets to the edge of town. Then through twisting, narrow, country roads bordered by mossy drystone walls. A fox crossed in front of the taxi, its eyes glowing white as they reflected the headlights. On the hunt for roosting birds or voles for supper.

Eventually they stopped at a pub set in, what appeared to Janet, the middle of nowhere. As they climbed out of the cab, Janet felt the chill of the wind, blowing fiercely without the shelter of other buildings to lessen its strength. The pub was on a high road, out in the countryside, with the twinkling lights of the town shining prettily in the valley below.

Janet could hear the music and laughter coming from inside the pub, despite the roar of the wind as Darren grabbed hold of her hand and led her through the old, timber door. Immediately, the wind and the cold disappeared, replaced by the comforting warmth of a packed pub with a roaring open fire.

"What do you want to drink?" asked Darren. Janet asked for her favourite cider.

"Two pints of Dark Fruits, ta," Darren asked the bearded barman, holding up two fingers in case the noise of the pub drowned out his order.

Drinks poured, they found a small, dark wood table in a quieter corner.

"It's busy in here!" said Janet surprised.

"Yeah, there's live music on Friday's, so it attracts a lot of custom," Darren explained,"My mates band are playing later."

Janet took a sip of her drink. She liked the atmosphere of the pub. It was as far from a trendy town centre pub as you could imagine. The clientele were all ages and the dress code appeared distinctly casual. She could see the purple cheeks and noses of the older men standing at the bar, laughing loudly at some joke or other. She guessed that they spent most evenings stood at that bar, drinking their pints and putting the world to rights.

There were younger people too, all laughing and chatting away. Janet soon found herself joining Darren in conversation herself, laughing and joking as they downed their pints.

"Another?" asked Darren, when their glasses were empty.

"I'll get these," insisted Janet. She was going to make sure she paid her way. She went to the bar, waiting with her card until the barman was free.

"Two pints of Dark Fruits please," Janet asked and paid with her card, before carrying them back to their table.

"Ta," said Darren grinning before taking a gulp, "Band should be on in a few minutes."

The bands equipment was already set up against the opposite wall of the pub. Big, black speakers, a drum kit and a few microphones on stands at different angles.

Janet sipped her drink. It tasted lovely and cool, just the way she liked it. She was really enjoying Darren's company and feeling relaxed and happy.

Three young men, dressed in jeans and t-shirts took their positions on the makeshift performance area. Darren took a last big gulp of his cider before standing, walking over and sitting behind the drum kit. Janet watched him with a confused expression and then laughed in happy surprise as he took up his sticks, grinning at her.

The band began their set. It was loud, it was raw, but it was so good! Strong basslines and entrancing melodies filled the little pub. Heads nodded in time to the beat as the lead singer, grasped the microphone in one hand and began belting out the lyrics in a powerful, captivating voice with an impressive range.

By the time the set ended, Janet found herself standing and clapping enthusiastically.

A smiling, sweaty Darren put down his sticks and made his way over to rejoin Janet. He took his seat and took a couple of huge swigs from his glass.

"That was so good" laughed Janet, "I didn't even know you played drums!"

The remaining band members came over and Darren introduced them to Janet. For the rest of the evening, more cider was consumed and conversation flowed freely among the group.

The last orders bell rang, and Darren phoned for a taxi. Saying their goodbyes to the others, the couple made their way outside. The wind hit them with force as they left the little pub and the cold air stung their cheeks.

"I've had such a good night," said Janet smiling, her eyes shining with excitement and the effects of four pints of cider.

Darren grinned, "Me too. We need to do this again."

Janet nodded in agreement and felt Darren's hand softly cupping her cold cheek. She looked into his green eyes. Suddenly serious, he pulled her close and they shared their first, lingering kiss. Slightly breathless, their eyes locked and Janet felt he was almost looking into her very soul, his gaze felt so intense. The spell was broken only by the headlights of their approaching taxi, its wheels crunching over the rough gravel of the carpark.

They held hands throughout the drive home, and chattered away as if they'd known each other forever. One final kiss goodbye, and a smiling Janet almost skipped up to her front door.

Inside, her grandma heard the key in the lock, put down her mug of tea on the small glass coffee and waited expectantly.

"Well?" grandma asked, "How did it go?"

Janet's smile told her all she needed to know before she'd uttered a single word.

Chapter Ten. Back to Work.

Cheryl was typing up the sales figures in the office. She'd plugged in the little, portable electric heater as the morning was chilly and damp. The one bar glowed a vivid orange but did little to remove the chill from her forty eight year old bones. Her manicured, scarlet fingernails tip tapped on the keyboard as she worked, purple framed glasses perched on the end of her pink, snub nose. Around her shoulders, was draped a lilac, fine knit cardigan and a hot lemon drink sat on her desk, steam rising. Every few seconds, she dabbed at her nose with a balled up tissue she kept up the sleeve of her white blouse.

Cheryl looked up at the wall clock, seven twenty five. She wished she was in bed, with a hot water bottle and a good book. She wouldn't say no to some nice, dark chocolate too, but no, she had to be in work. She couldn't afford not to be.

Darren was positively buzzing as he got to work. With a new spring in his step, he entered the office, smiling at Cheryl, the P.A. to the big boss. "Someone looks like the cat that got the cream," said Cheryl with a raise of an elegantly shaped eyebrow.

"Just happy to be alive on a beautiful day," Darren replied with a wink as he collected the orders. Frowning, Cheryl looked out of the window at the rain, sheeting down outside, "Beautiful day?" she muttered to herself as Darren left the office for the warehouse floor. Liam was there already picking his first order. Mohammed was on his second. Janet appeared from the staff room and beamed a welcome smile. Liam didn't miss the subtle change in their interactions throughout the morning and when Darren left to go back to the office, he drew Janet to one side.

"Janet," he began, in his strong Croatian accent, "I can see you and Darren are getting closer. It's not my business, I know. But be very, very careful. He is bad news."

Janet just looked at Liam for a second, before laughing saying, "Nooo, he's a good lad. A bit on the cheeky side, but nothing to worry about."

Liam's face remained serious, "He is not a good man at all. Just keep yourself safe. Please."

Janet stood puzzled for a moment as Liam turned and returned to his work, then shrugged her shoulders as she dismissed his warning as some kind of miscommunication due to English not being Liam's first language.

Darren returned to the warehouse, oblivious to the altercation and continued his picking and packing, whistling to himself.

Liam also carried on working, but all the while worrying about Janet. She was a good girl, worked hard, a good mother to her children. He didn't want her to get herself involved with Darren, to be influenced by him down a dark path. Brow furrowed, Liam worked silently, but he was not happy with the situation. Not happy at all.

The bell rang for lunch. Darren went straight outside for a smoke. Cheryl was there already, with hunched shoulders, shivering as she drew on her cigarette. It was a miserable day as he huddled under the designated smoking shelter with the others getting their fix of nicotine.

Raindrops tapped noisily on the corrugated tin roof then fell in riverlets off the edges like some curtain of clear crystal beads.

It was a grey day. Grey clouds full of grey rain falling onto grey slate rooftops and grey concrete slab pavements.

Like beasts in some nature documentary, with shoulders hunched up around their ears, the herd of smokers blew grey smoke into the grey drizzle. Stamping their hooves to extinguish their cigarettes, as one, the herd moved indoors to eat.

Janet was already sat in the staffroom, tupperware box open in front of her, eating her tuna mayo sandwich. Mohammed's food was heating in the little microwave.

Darren grabbed his cellophane wrapped pasty, and his can of pepsi, from the fridge and sat across from Janet. Janet could feel Liam's eyes on them. It made her feel uncomfortable. Trying to ignore it, she chatted away to Darren. He asked her over to his for a meal at the weekend, and she said she'd see if her grandma would babysit again. "Or, if it's easier, I could come over to yours?" he suggested. "Ok. I'll cook for you," she offered smiling.

"It's a date!" he replied, "I'll bring the beers."

The microwave pinged and Mohammed came to join them and the conversation soon turned to football and what should be done to improve Burnleys chances in the new season. Everyone was an expert when it came to the fortunes of their beloved team and they discussed strategy, transfers, who was playing well, who should be on the subs bench in great detail until the bell signalled a return to work.

Chapter Eleven. Greta.

Greta bounced out of the gym, smiling to herself, and with a spring in her step. On a dopamine high, and feeling positively puritanical drinking from her water bottle, she was thinking about dinner. Maybe baked salmon and a green salad? Or prawns?
Still wearing her gym outfit of grey three quarter length leggings, grey t-shirt, lilac zip up hoody and white and pink trainers she was too pumped to notice the slight chill in the air. She jogged toward the car park, her high pony tail swinging to and fro with each footfall. Darkness had crept in unnoticed as Greta had pounded out the miles on the treadmill. It was mid September and the nights were drawing in. The moon was full but clouds prevented the majority of its luminescence reaching the earth below.
Ms. Greta Grey was a successful solicitor; young, beautiful, healthy and financially independent. She had everything going for her and shedloads of ambition to boot. She was single, not for want of admirers, but because she chose to be. She didn't need the complications of a relationship. Life was good for Greta, her future was looking extremely bright and she was content.
The street lamps in front of the car park cast pools of sodium yellow light, transforming the colours of the cars parked beneath them to various shades of brown. Spots of rain began to fall, slowly at first, but getting heavier by the second. Greta pulled up the hood of her sweat jacket.
Almost at her car, she pressed the key button and heard the familiar clunk of the door unlocking, accompanied by a flash of the headlights as if the shiny, graphite grey, Audi Quattro was greeting her on her return.

As her hand clasped the door handle, she felt a white hot pain shoot through her skull and then the world suddenly went black, as Greta collapsed to the ground, out cold.

Chapter Twelve. A bit of peace.

The night was cold. Not just chilly, not just the 'make sure your coat's buttoned up' kind of cold, but a bitter, fresh off the pennines cold.

The kind of cold that chills to the bone, that numbs the feeling in feet and fingers as the body diverts its blood supply to major organs. So cold that your tongue would be instantly frozen fast to metal should you be stupid enough to lick it.

Cats were far from stupid. Tonight they stayed outside just long enough to pee and then dashed home to stretch and sleep, sprawled on rugs in front of orange gas fires.

Dog walkers cut short their excursions in favour of curling up on comfy sofas with hot chocolate and BBC dramas. Their dogs, lying on their backs with floppy legs, oblivious of their obscene poses.

If you had looked, straight up, into the clear sky you would see the darkest midnight blue, dotted with a myriad stars like tiny diadems on velvet. Then, the waxing moon, suspended low in the navy sky, glowing softly, casting its gentle, blue-white luminescence, giving the hills and the town an eerie, ethereal feel.

Decorations were beginning to appear in houses and shop displays as September turned into October, the month of Halloween. Plastic and rubber skeletons, cotton handkerchief ghosts and gossamer cobwebs made from man-made fibres in Chinese sweatshops, hung garishly suspended in windows.

Behind the yellow light of double glazed house windows, children pestered their parents for over priced, neon and black costumes, before being sent to bed, dreaming of gravestones, ghouls and glow-in-the-dark ghosts.

Harry and Amy were tucked up in their beds, too young to dream of Halloween. They lay, mouths open, fingers curled, long eyelashes resting on rosy cheeks. Secure, safe and sound asleep. Their dreams, full of innocence and ice cream.

The little house was silent, barring the low hum of the boiler, feeding the central heating and keeping a constant, cosy warmth throughout the rooms.

Janet was making use of her 'me' time by having a long, relaxing soak in the bath. She wasn't seeing Darren tonight. She liked time spent in her own company to balance out time spent with others. Smiling to herself, Janet realised that for the first time in ages, she felt happy and content. Eyes closed, she lay back in the bath, her silver hair piled up out of the way in a twisted bun.

Feeling indulgent, she'd added a capful of the far too expensive, moisturising bath oil that Darren had recently surprised her with as a gift. The copious amount of fine, silky bubbles it created smelled luxuriously of ylang-ylang and bergamot. Both of these essential oils were known to reduce stress and anxiety and already her breathing had slowed alongside her heart rate.

She inhaled the calming scent that drifted from lavender tea-lights, their flickering, soft, incandescence further enhancing the soothing ambience of the small bathroom.

As she lay there, enjoying the sensual, almost therapeutic stimulation of all five of her senses, her mind wandered to Darren. Her affection for him was growing by the day and she could see a time, in the not too distant future, that she might start to call that affection love. Her defensive walls, built high after her disastrous relationship with the father of her children, were beginning to crumble. She'd found Darren to be funny, caring, patient, giving and damn sexy.

But one thing that was still troubling her was Liam, and his warning. She had seen absolutely nothing wrong in Darren's character or the way he conducted himself when he was with her. It niggled her. Was she missing something?

As a cautious and protective mother, the last thing she wanted was to bring a man into their lives to spoil things. The children came first, always. No man was worth risking their safety and happiness.

Janet frowned. What was Liam's motive? Was he jealous? She didn't think so. They were very different people and he'd never given the slightest indication of any romantic intentions. She mulled over a thousand and one reasons in her mind for Liam's words of warning, but nothing seemed to fit.

After a great deal of pondering and over thinking, she decided Liam had just been mistaken. Her judgement of people was generally pretty accurate and Darren had been nothing but considerate, but that little seed of doubt would stay in some far corner of her mind, keeping her vigilant for any negative signs in their relationship.

Janet stepped out of her bath, dried herself with a turquoise bath sheet and dressed in cosy, checked flannelette pyjamas before getting into her bed with a steaming mug of coffee and a good book to read.

Chapter Thirteen. Majke.

It was a mild, unremarkable day. Neither warm nor cold. Neither clear nor cloudy. Neither wet nor dry. Just a vaguely damp, colourless, nondescript kind of day in September. The sun seemed too melancholy to shine any brighter than a wan, watery-white, lukewarm light over the landscape and the wind was too lethargic to blow. Grey birds sat on grey rooves set against a grey sky. Grey people walked along grey pavements to dull jobs that took the best years of their dull lives.

She was dead. Her skin, the insipid, sickly pallor of Campbells chicken soup. Her lips, paler than candlewax. He'd found her this morning. She'd slipped quietly away in her sleep. No fanfare, no grand gestures, no tears or cries of pain, no dramatic death rattle. Just an ordinary, unremarkable death on an ordinary, unremarkable day.

Now, he was truly alone. No brothers, no sisters, not even any cousins he was aware of.

Liam was now an orphan.

Completely alone.

He sat by her iron framed bed, on the old dining chair she used as a nightstand. Its worn, dove tailed joints creaked with age as he shifted his weight.

Praying silently for her soul as he held her small, hand, he noticed the liver spots and the blue veins visible through the thin, pale skin. He saw the palm, worn rough by years of work; scrubbing, cleaning, sewing and cooking. There were the small scars, from knife slips as she was peeling countless hard root vegetables throughout the decades, and from the burns, suffered through years of sliding hot dishes on and off oven shelves.

These were the hands that carried him as an infant, that soothed and comforted him as a child, that calmed him when he was afraid, that cared for him when he was sick and that brought him nourishment, right up until today.

"Majka," said Liam softly, "Bog te blagoslovio, lijevo spavaj." which, in Croatian, meant, 'Mother, God bless you, sleep well.'

He gently placed her hand back by her side and phoned for the doctor.

After the men from the chapel of rest had taken his mother's body, he stripped her bed, putting the timeworn flannelette sheets and pillowcases into the washing machine.

Next, he phoned the warehouse, telling them that he wouldn't be in today as his mother had died. Giving him her sincere condolences, Cheryl told him not to worry, to not return to work until he felt ready and that she would let Mohammed know.

Then he took the juniper shoots from the little vase on the window sill and threw them in the bin. He took a damp cloth and wiped the salt from the lintels, he cut off the knotted strands of red wool from her bedstead and threw those in the bin also. He took the cloves of garlic he'd carried for protection from his pockets, he no longer needed them. He removed every sign of his Vlach heritage from his home.

Then he showered, washing his hair and every inch of his skin, purifying himself.

Stepping out of the shower, he walked naked into the living room. He felt free! Free to fully embrace his destiny, to feel the power of the One True God flowing through him without encumbrance. He raised up his hands in supplication and sank to his knees,

"Lord, your servant is ready,

Bless him with strength and wisdom and let his thoughts be fixed on You.

Use him as a means to heal the earth and stamp out wickedness."

He felt himself grow hard. He was tempted to stroke the rigid shaft, to bring himself to release, but no. He was a servant of God, not a slave to the flesh.

Liam methodically searched through the kitchen drawers. Finding the ball of twine, he cut off a length of around a metre, and began binding his shaft to his balls, winding the string tight. He continued until he reached the end of the twine and then knotted it firmly. The twine constricted his balls, leaving them smooth and pink like two curled up baby mice, and his penis trussed up tight. The pain was intense, but necessary he thought as he sat down, still naked, to read his bible in his favourite chair.

Chapter Fourteen.
Condolence.

It was a busy day in the factory. The air had a distinct autumnal nip and the workers had begun to pull out their winter knitwear and thick socks for work. The concrete floor was cold underfoot, despite the thick soles of the steel toe capped boots they were obligated to wear, and they soon felt the chill.

Janet walked purposefully over to Mohammed with a pen and an open greetings card with hands partly covered by woolly fingerless gloves. Liam's mum had died two day's ago and Janet had appointed herself in charge of buying a condolence card. She was now making the rounds amongst her workmates, asking them if they'd like to sign it. Liam had been given time off work and they were all thinking of him.

"Alright Mo, I've got Liam's card if you want to sign it?" she said, holding out the card and her pen.

Mohammed stopped working, wiped imaginary dirt from his palms on his trousers and began to write,

'To Liam, so sorry to hear of the death of your mum. Our prayers are with you, Mo.'

"Thanks Mo," she said and walked across to Tariq.

Sealing the parcel with a packing tape gun, Mohammed went to collect more orders from the office.

"Hello Cheryl, how are you this fine afternoon? " Mohammed said cheerily.

Cheryl Hargraves looked up from her desktop computer smiling, "Not too bad, though I'll be a helluva lot better at five o'clock!"

Cheryl stretched, arms over her head, sticking out her ample bosom as she did so. Mohammed might be mistaken, but he had a feeling that might have been the reason for the stretch. The lace of her bra was clearly visible through the thin material of her white blouse.

He'd caught her smiling at him more recently. She lived on her own, well with a yappie pomeranian, but no husband. She'd told him that herself, casually mentioning that it could get lonely. He found it quite a complement that she was showing an interest in him. It was flattering, but he loved his wife dearly and would never put his marriage at risk.

Mohammed picked up the stack of orders and left Cheryl to her typing, the noise of Cheryl's long, painted nails tip tapping away as she worked. He passed Janet on her way to the office with Liams card and they smiled at each other as they crossed paths.

"Hi Cheryl," said Janet, "I've brought the condolence card for Liam. Want to sign it?"

Cheryl looked up, "Course I will, poor man. He lived with his mum didn't he?" she said taking the pen from Janet's hand.

Janet nodded, "Yes. She wasn't that old really either, early fifties perhaps?"

"That's no age these days!" replied Cheryl, who wasn't far off that age herself. "It must have come as quite a shock. I might pop round one evening, take him some food."

"That's kind of you," Janet said smiling.

Cheryl smiled back, "You've got to do what you can, don't you?"

Janet wondered cynically if she would be as forthcoming if Liam wasn't a fairly good looking single man. Janet smiled to herself, she found Cheryl's poor attempts at attracting a man quite amusing, but also a little sad. She was a lovely lady though, thought Janet, if she didn't come across as so desperate, she might have more success. That was up to Cheryl though, and Janet very much doubted that Cheryl would ever change. Cheryl was Cheryl, and everybody loved her for that.

Janet left the small office as Cheryl brought up Liam's details to find out his home address.

Sealing up a box, Darren was putting the label on the front when Tariq came over. "So Darren," he began, "You and Janet, you together then?"

Darren grinned, "It's beginning to look that way."

"Good on ya man. She's a nice looking girl and you look good together," said Tariq, playfully punching Darren's arm, "Get in there!"

Darren laughed, "What about you Tariq, anyone you got your eye on?"

"Nah," Tariq replied, "I'm not getting tied down just yet, am too young for all that. Keeping my options open."

Darren had the distinct impression that Tariq preferred male company rather than female, though Tariq had never spoken about his sexuality. Darren was aware, however, that in Tariq's religion, being gay was an incredibly difficult thing to reconcile. At only eighteen, there were enough hang ups and anxieties without the added pressure of such a big secret. Darren couldn't be one hundred percent sure, but he hoped that Tariq would figure himself out and find love and a good future, whatever, with whoever and wherever that may be. All Darren could do, was be a good friend, and be there for Tariq if he ever needed him.

The two men continued their picking and packing, and soon, Janet was back.

Tariq grinned at her, "It's about time you two got together," he said, "Me and Mo had a bet on about you both. I said you'd be together by October first, he said by Christmas, so I'm quids in!"

Janet opened her mouth in mock shock, "Cheeky bugger!" she said laughing, and asked Darren to sign the card.

After everyone had signed the card, Janet added her own message, sealed it up and put Liam's address on the front, ready for posting on the way home.

Chapter Fifteen. Shepherd's Pie.

Cheryl Marie Hargraves hummed a tune to herself in her pastel pink kitchen as she finely chopped an onion. Her eyes began to sting, but she soldiered on.

Sizzling as it hit the hot pan, the minced lamb browned as Cheryl stirred, breaking it up with a wooden spoon so no pink flesh remained. She then added the chopped onions, stirring until they turned translucent and soft. Poppet sniffed the air, his acute canine sense of smell telling him food was near. Cheryl added stock and seasoning and let the meat simmer as she put the potatoes on to boil.

Leaving the two saucepans to bubble away on the hob, Cheryl opened a tin of dogfood for Poppet, the Pomeranian. With a gloopy squelch, the meat and gravy slid out of the tin into a pale pink, ceramic bowl, with 'Poppet' hand painted in white on the side. The little dog came scampering over as soon as he heard the metallic scraping of the fork on the tin, and began to eat greedily.

After transferring the meat to a rectangular pyrex dish, she mashed the now soft potatoes, spooned them over the mince and took her time adding a ridged heart pattern on the surface with the back of a fork. Everyone likes a shepherd's pie she thought to herself, and the way to a man's heart is through his stomach.

She put the pyrex dish under the grill and washed up the pots she'd used as she waited for it to brown.

After it had cooled slightly, she carefully covered it with aluminium foil and left it on the worktop, and then let Poppet out into the back garden.

Whilst the dog sniffed around outside and did his business, Cheryl went into her bedroom, where she spritzed her favourite perfume into the air and stepped, eyes closed, into its mist.

Back in the kitchen, "Poppet," she called musically into the darkness of the back garden until the little black and white dog reappeared and trotted back inside.

Gazing at her reflection in the hallway mirror, she applied a fresh coat of passionate pink to her lips, dabbed powder to remove the oil shine on her nose and quickly brushed her auburn hair. Happy with the result, she picked up her bag and car keys and called, "Back soon Poppet," to the little black and white dog, who was now asleep on the rug. His ears pricked up, but his eyes remained firmly closed, he was far too comfortable to move.

Slipping on her coat and holding the shepherds pie level so as not to spill any of the gravy onto her clothes, Cheryl went outside to her purple Renault clio.

It was a still night, quiet as the grave she thought to herself as she started the engine. The moon was full in the cloudless sky lending a silver sheen to the glossy leaves of her laurel hedge as she backed out of her driveway.

A short while later, she parked her little car outside of Liam's house. The car door shut with a clunk that echoed slightly as she carried the shepherd's pie carefully up the path to the front door.

Cheryl knocked on the door thinking how quiet the streets were tonight. Ahh she thought, the penny suddenly dropping, it's because of the murder. A friendly, black cat rubbed itself against her legs as she stood waiting.

"Hello lovely," she said, bending down and tickling the cat behind it's ears.

Just then, the red front door opened and Liam stood silhouetted and barefoot.

"Hello Liam love. Is this little fella yours? began Cheryl pointing to the little cat.

Liam looked puzzled," Er, no, not mine." "Am so sorry to hear about your poor mother," said Cheryl, cocking her head to one side sympathetically, "I've brought you some tea, shall I warm it up for you," she continued as she walked inside Liam's home without waiting to be invited.

Liam closed the door and followed her to the kitchen.

The cat, left outside and alone, wandered leisurely back down the path, but then suddenly sank down low, its eyes fixed at a point in the grass verge. Shoulder blades raised, belly almost touching the ground. Imperceptibly slowly, the cat moved forward, each shoulder falling and rising in turn with each step. A raise of one forepaw, then stillness, not a muscle moving, eyes fixed, then the paw ever so slowly descends, weight shifts and he's one step closer. Almost there now, the other paw raises, a tremor of his haunches and he leaps forward, pouncing onto the tiny shrew in the grass. He has it within his paws.

With its near dead prey hanging from its mouth, the black cat slinks silently away into the darkness.

Chapter Sixteen. Alone.

Two days later, he was at the cemetery. The sky was silver and platinum, with altostratus sheets of cloud glittering with ice crystal diamonds.

He stood alone at her graveside, next to the mound of mud and sticky clay, the sterile sub soil, the dead zone that holds no life. Holding his cap in his large hands, he stood, looking down on his dead mother, packed inside a dead tree box and lain in the dead ground.

There was no one else there. He needed no one else.

She was all he had and he was all she had.

He threw in a handful of earth, then nodded to the waiting grave diggers to signal them to beging filling in the grave.

There would be no headstone, nor marker. Not even a single flower. He would never return to his mother's grave.

'Let the dead, bury the dead,' he quoted to himself the words of Jesus. He had more important matters to attend to. Walking slowly away, he felt different. Something new ran through his veins, like fire. Something powerful.

"I am ready, Father," he spoke into the wind and the wind answered, "Yes, my son."

Back at the warehouse, Mohammed was feeling stressed. He knew Liam needed a day off for his mother's funeral, but now Cheryl was off sick with an ear infection and the temp brought in had no idea how the system worked. In the end, the big boss gave the temp some typing to do, and manned the orders himself. It was chaos for a while but they were gradually getting back on track.

Darren, Janet and Tariq were doing a sterling job but they were still playing catch up and had to keep a good pace. Tariq had really upped his game, he hadn't needed a nudge all day.

At least all this running about was keeping him warm, thought Mohammed. His cold was almost gone and he really hoped he hadn't given it anyone else. The last thing he needed was anyone else off sick.

He would phone Nasreen during his break and ask her to make some of her tasty samosas that he could bring into work to keep up morale. Mohammed always thought of his team and was proud of them. They were almost a little family to him and he enjoyed making them feel a valued part of the business.

He suddenly had an idea. There was a part tub of 'Celebrations' in the office. Everyone likes a bit of chocolate, he thought. Nipping quickly through to get the tub, Mohammed returned and offered everyone the chocolate. The smiles told him he'd made a good decision. A happy team is a productive team, he said to himself.

Chapter Seventeen. The Discovery.

"Some kids found her. They're pretty shook up," the young policeman, PC Ibrahim Choudary, explained to DI Johnson, who was stood staring at the corpse below.

"Ok. Do you want to take some details from them, and we'll contact the parents before we take formal statements," the DI instructed the younger policeman. PC Choudary nodded and went over to the young teenagers.

The rain had finally stopped but the ground was a quagmire of mud and sodden, yellow, autumn leaves from the self seeded ash trees dotted around the area. A small stream ran through the dip in the landscape, swollen slightly by the heavy rain. In summer it would be barely a trickle.

Ian Johnson pulled at his grey, suit trousers above the knees and crouched down on his haunches for a closer look at the corpse. Her dark hair was scraped tightly back into a high ponytail revealing her pale face, with open, cyanotic lips devoid of any trace of rosiness, any trace of life. Her face was grotesquely bloated and mottled blue. Between the lips, writhing and squirming, were hundreds of creamy white larvae. The smell of the maggots and putrefaction made the policeman's nose wrinkle in distaste. He would never get used to that smell. Like faeces, but sweeter with notes of boiled cabbage. Her thin, grey t-shirt was stretched tight over her chest from the build up of gases and fluids within her tissues. Straw coloured liquid with ruddy streaks had oozed out from her genitals, seeping through the grey material of her leggings and attracting the attention of insects. Her feet were in the water, still wearing the pink and white trainers from her gym visit.

Her fingers had dried blood on them and the nails were painted a vivid peacock green. With their perfect, manicured gloss, the appearance of the nails seemed to jar obscenely with the dirty, repulsive state of her body. A large moonstone ring adorned the middle finger of her right hand.

DS Abdul Rasheed came over and stood next to the DI.

"Any sign of I.D?" asked Johnson without looking up. The DS shook his head, "Nothing so far Sir, but we've got PC's White and Carpenter still searching the immediate area."

The DI took a biro and prodded at the label on the zip up hoody next to the body. "Clothes look more designer than bargain basement," he thought aloud, "Good manicure. Well cut hair with recent lowlights. Maybe a professional, or the wife of one? No wedding ring though."

DI Johnson scanned the body for a possible cause of death. No wounds immediately apparent. Accidental? Wouldn't have thought so, he mused.

He stood up and looked around. They were in a dip in the ground, more of a ditch than a dip. No litter suggested that people rarely came this way. No empty Strongbow cans or cigarette ends in sight. They were hidden from the road. No houses overlooking the spot. Perfect for dumping a body.

Ian left the body in the care of the SOCO's, DS Rasheed and the coroner with instructions for extending the cordon and search directions. In his polished work shoes with virtually no grip on the smooth soles, he clumsily climbed the steep slope made slippery with a layer of fallen leaves. Slipping and sliding, almost losing his balance a couple of times, Ian finally made it to the top.

Back at his car, he looked down at the mud on his shoes and trousers and sighed in irritation.

His phone buzzed. "DI Johnson," he said as he picked up.

"Sir, It's PC Preston. We've had a report of a car outside the St. Peter's Street Gym, three recent parking tickets on the windscreen, Audi Quattro, registered to a Greta Grey. 18 Stanmore Gardens. DOB 07/07/91," said the voice on the other end."

"That could well be our vic. Thanks for that Preston. I'll try the address."

By the next morning, the news was all over the town.

"Did you hear about the murder?" a shocked Janet asked Darren as she walked into the warehouse. It was early morning and Darren was first in the warehouse, closely followed by Tariq and Janet.

"What murder?" interrupted Tariq.

Janet was talking rapidly, unsettled by the news, "They found a woman's body, off Pike hill way, murdered, some teenagers found her. That must be horrible, finding a body. "

"I heard it on the radio on my way in," said Darren, "They don't know who she is yet."

Mohammed walked into the warehouse.

"Mo, did you hear about the murder?" asked Janet.

Mohammed sighed, "Terrible thing to happen. In Burnley too. The world is a cruel place sometimes."

Darren nodded.

"But they don't know who it is?" asked Tariq.

"Not yet, but I'm sure they'll find out soon," replied Mohammed.

Just then, Liam walked into the warehouse.

"Liam. Did you hear about the murder?"

Liam eyes widened, "Murder? What, in Burnley?"

Janet answered him, still finding it hard to believe, "The police said there's a woman's body, found by teenagers, up Pike Hill."

Liam just stood, not quite sure what to say.

"It's creepy thinking there's a murderer out there," said Janet, voicing her fears out loud.

"Try not to worry Janet," Liam reassured her, "These things are very rare."

"Still, I hope they catch whoever did it soon," she replied.

Darren and Tariq nodded in agreement.

"We've got a good police force in this country," said Mohammed, "With any luck, they'll have caught the killer by tea time. But for now, there's packing to be done. Chop, chop, let's get to work. Should have started five minutes ago!"

The little group dispersed and began picking the first orders of the day.

Chapter Eighteen. Spicy.

Smells of garlic, onions and spices filled the air in the modest terraced house. Janet stirred the simmering pot of chicken curry. The kids were upstairs asleep after their tea of fish fingers, chips and beans. This food was for the grown ups; herself and Darren. In the small, dining room, on the dark wood, laminate floor stood an old, circular, second hand table. Janet had placed a purple cotton, batik printed cloth over it. She lit two rose pink tea lights and placed them in glass holders on the table. Their flickering light made dancing shadows on the lavender coloured walls.

The thick, wine coloured curtains were drawn across the window to keep out the draught. Two small table lamps with wine coloured shades were lit on the junk shop find sideboard. Altogether, the room had a cosy, intimate feel, perfect for a romantic dinner for two. She opened a pack of shop bought poppadoms and placed them on a plate centrally on the table. Next to it, she placed a bowl of mango chutney and a spoon.

Outside, Darren was walking down Janet's street swinging a four pack of lager from one hand. The sky was clear which meant stars above and frost on the ground. The pavement twinkled with frosted ice crystals as he walked, giving it a magical, glittered quality. He wore a heavy winter coat and a checked scarf and his breath turned to vapour as soon as it left his mouth.

Arriving at Janet's house, he knocked on the pvc front door. After a moment, the door opened and Janet welcomed him into her home. Darren's glasses misted up with moisture as he went from the cold outside to the cosy, warmth of the house.

After removing his heavy coat, he took off his glasses and cleaned them with the end of his scarf.

"Brass monkeys out there," Darren said, replacing his glasses and handing the beer to Janet.

"Tell me about it," agreed Janet, "My feet were like blocks of ice waiting in that playground for the kids to come out of after school club,"

Darren put a cold hand on the back of her neck, making her let out a little scream, before he pulled her close and kissed her. She responded and wound her arms around his neck and molded her body against him.

" Missed you," said Darren.

" You only saw me a few hours ago, you daft beggar," she laughed, getting out two glasses for their beers.

They ate dinner, with plenty of laughter and easy conversation. After shop bought ice cream for dessert, Janet suggested taking their next drinks into the living room.

Flames flickered in the log burning stove as they sat comfortably on the tan sofa, listening to music. She leant against his chest and he had his arm around her shoulder. His other hand held his near empty glass of beer.

The scent of her hair mixed with her perfume, filled his nostrils.

"You do make a good chicken curry," said Darren, feeling full and content. He put his glass on the small side table and tilted her chin. He looked into her wide eyes and kissed her gently. She responded, pressing her lips harder against his, her toungue exploring the warmth of his mouth. He kissed her now with more urgency, hungry for the taste of her. Feeling his cock begin to stir, his hands began to explore her body as they kissed. He cupped one full breast in his hand and felt her nipple grow erect as his thumb played on her skin. She let out a low groan and her hand moved slowly towards his jeans, finally feeling the hardness of him beneath the denim. Feeling the length of him excited her further and she felt the heat between her legs. He lifted her shirt over her head and off, revealing the black lace of her bra. He sank his face between her breasts, kissing them softly, before lifting the flimsy fabric over them and using his tongue to tease her pink nipples. He pulled on her maxi skirt, the elasticated waist making it easy for him to slide it the whole way down her legs. He saw her black, lace knickers, his eyes drinking her in. He slowly removed them, opened her legs and began soft butterfly kisses on the inside of her thigh. His tongue trailed across from her thigh to her mound, then dipped into it and began licking her clitoris with short, firm strokes. Her hips rose and she groaned with pleasure as he flicked his tongue repeatedly over the swollen bud. He breathed in the musky scent of her sex as he worked her, his cock fully hard now. He stood and quickly removed his t-shirt and then his jeans. His cock stood erect and Janet's eyes glittered. He gazed over her, naked except for the black boots. He took a condom packet out of his jeans.

"Here, let me," she said, kneeling. She ripped open the packet. Noticing the drop of precum appear from his hard cock, she removed it with a flick of her tongue before sliding the condom slowly down the full length of his shaft.

"Lie down," she instructed hoarsly, and Darren laid down on the thick rug. Kneeling astride of him, she slowly lowered herself onto him as he let out a low moan. She slowly began to move, sliding herself up to the tip of his cock and then down deep to the base. His mouth was open, his eyes fixed on her body as she moved. She licked her lips and began to move faster, his hips rising to meet her downward strokes. Faster she went, slick with juices, her breathing ragged. Her eyes closed, her head tilted back, back arched and she came, ripples of liquid fire coursing through her. He thrust twice more inside her before his own orgasm began to explode with a loud groan accompanying the strong pulses of his release.

Janet collapsed to the side of him, resting her head on his chest as she slowly recovered.

Darren kissed the top of her head his breathing beginning to return to its normal rate.

They lay there together, silently bathing in the afterglow of their union, the fire warm on their skin and the contentment that comes with true togetherness.

Chapter Nineteen. Loss.

DI Johnson and PC Jagpal Randhawa walked up the lavender bordered path to the white painted door of the impressive, detached, stone built property. Pink climbing roses still bloomed against the wall of the house softening it's appearance. Johnson rapped the brass door knocker. As he waited for an answer, Ian admired the cottage style planting of the front garden, bathed in September sunshine. Lavender blue clumps of asters, willowy, candy pink and pure white japanese anenomes with yellow centres, daisy-like, pink echinaceas and pom pom dahlias in various shades of wine and deep pinks.

An white-haired man of around seventy, slightly stooped, answered the door.

DI Johnson flashed his police identity card, "Police. May we come in Mr Grey?"

With his face wrinkling into a puzzled expression, the man opened the door wider and beckoned them in.

Mr Grey led the two officers through an elegant entrance hall with a heavy, half moon table set against one wall on which were deep purple gladioli in a tall crystal vase.

They entered a large, living room with dusky pink and beige, patterned carpet and pink, floral wallpaper. A large, picture window framed a view of the extensive, ornamental back garden. The furniture was antique, polished cherrywood and a white plaster, Adams style fireplace dominated one wall. A woman in her early sixties sat on the pink velour suite with her slippered feet raised up on a matching pouffe.

"It's the police Mary," said the old man as he entered the room. He motioned for the two officers to sit on the pink sofa.

"Police?" repeated Mary, "What's happened?"

Her husband, Charles, lowered himself slowly into the remaining armchair and waited for DI Johnson to explain the purpose of his visit.

"Mr and Mrs Grey?" he began. The couple nodded.

"The parents of Greta Grey?" he continued. Another nod.

"I'm afraid I have some bad news. Greta was found dead today," he said gently.

Mary gasped and both her hands rose up to her mouth, "Greta? Our Greta?"

Charles just stared at the policeman with a frown of confusion.

"I'm afraid, we suspect foul play," finished DI Johnson.

"Murder?" asked Mary, incredulously, "Greta has been murdered?"

"Am so sorry," replied the DI, "But yes. PC Randhawa, could you please make Mr and Mrs Grey some tea?"

Jagpal immediately stood up and went to find the kitchen, part of her glad to escape the sorrowful scene in the living room, another part guilty for feeling that way.

Finding the kitchen, PC Randhawa, boiled the kettle and made tea in two china cups. She found a tray for the cups, placed them on it and carried it back down the hall.

"... everything in our power to catch whoever did this," Jagpal heard the end of the DI's sentence as she opened the door to the living room She placed the tray on the oval coffee table with curved, Queen Anne legs.

The couple were sat together on the sofa now, still shocked and struggling to comprehend the awful news.

PC Randhawa sat quietly in the newly vacated armchair.

DI Johnson continued to gently ask the couple questions about their only daughter's lifestyle. The officers listened as the couple spoke of Gretas success in her practise as a solicitor. No, they didn't know of any enemies. She was very work motivated, but did find time for the gym and meeting her friends. She liked to read, particularly about alternative therapies and ancient philosophies and was a member of some group or other of like minded people.

After almost an hour of talking, the two officers left the couple with their deepest condolences, plus Jagpal's number as assigned family liason, and a bereavement helpline card. Mr Grey saw them out and softly closed the door. He could hear his wife's sobs as he slowly made his way back to the living room, feeling far older than he had when he awoke that day.

"Never gets any easier, does it PC Randhawa?" sighed Ian as he closed the car door and turned the ignition.

"No, it's very sad," she agreed, fastening her seatbelt, "One visit, and their whole world is changed."

"Makes you count your blessings," answered the DI as he indicated, then pulled away from the Grey house, "Got to make the most of life. You never know when it's going to end."

Jagpal nodded in agreement, knowing she would hug her two children a little tighter that night, after her shift was over and she went home.

Chapter Twenty.
Connections.

Eve had made herself a mug of green tea to sip as she took a leisurely look through the newspaper. She was having a relaxed morning wearing a patterned silk, kimono style robe and her feet were bare.

"LOCAL SOLICITOR SLAIN"

A full colour picture of a serious looking Greta Grey, looking very professional in a smart, designer suit, was printed underneath the headline.

Eve read through the full piece. Despite living in a largely digital age, Eve still liked to read the news in a real newspaper. She liked the feel and the smell of a newspaper, and the way she could read at her own pace, without having to wait for pages to load or adverts to finish playing.

'Local solicitor, Ms. Greta Grey, 26, was found dead on wasteland yesterday, after going missing following a visit to the St. Peters Street Gym on Friday evening. Her metallic 2019, grey Audi Quattro was found abandoned in the gym car park and it is believed she met her attacker shortly after leaving the gym.

Fellow solicitor, Mr Grahame Higson, stated that, "Ms. Grey was a well respected partner in the business and a valued friend. Our thoughts are with her family at this sad time."

Police at present have no solid leads. If you have any information regarding this case, or the whereabouts of Ms. Grey between 8pm on Friday the thirteenth of September and the morning of Thursday the nineteenth, please contact the police on…'

The phone started playing the little tune that told her Yasmin was calling. "Hello", said Eve. "Hi mum. Did you read about the murder?" Yasmin asked worriedly.

"Yes, really terrible. Your father's working on the case, " answered Eve.

"Rose knew her!" her daughter said in a shocked voice, "She was a regular customer at Pagan Paraphernalia."

"Oh my!" replied Eve with genuine concern, "Did she know her well?"

"Pretty well, yes," said Yasmine, "Rose said she was always in, buying little bits and having a coffee."

Rose's little café and shop in Hebden Bridge had a loyal following of regular customers buying incense, candles, pagan books, jewellery etc.

Mother and daughter chatted away, discussing Gretas murder before moving onto less unsavoury topics.

" Are you and Rose still coming over for late lunch on your dad's birthday? asked Eve, "I've asked your brother and Molly too."

" Ooo yes, Of course we're coming," replied Yasmin," It's a Sunday, so the shop will be closed. "

"Good!" said Eve happily, "We'll see you around three."

"Great!" Yasmin answered, "See you then. Love you, bye."

"Bye," replied Eve before she pressed the red phone to end the call. Her tea was now cold, so she poured it down the sink and put the kettle back on to boil.

Eve shivered although it wasn't particularly cold, she felt unnerved by the murder. She hated violence and found it incredibly sad that someone could deliberately inflict pain and suffering on another in cold blood.

The kettle boiled and she poured the boiling water onto the teabag in her mug.

Gazing out of the window whilst the tea brewed, she saw the green feathers of a woodpecker as it landed on the little bird table in the garden. He was a beautiful bird. With his scarlet red head, chartreuse green back and black mask over his bead like eyes, he was one of the most colourful of native British birds. Eve smiled to herself. There may be ugliness in the world, but there was also great beauty to be found everywhere.

She took the teabag out of her mug and sipped her tea as she watched the green bird jump down onto the lawn to look for beetles among the blades of grass.

Other, smaller birds kept a respectful distance as he searched. Eve kept watching him until finally he flew up into the trees and disappeared from view.

She sighed and decided it was probably time to get dressed, ready for her art classes this afternoon at the college. Draining the last of her tea, she ascended the stairs to shower and change for work.

Chapter TwentyOne.
Funeral.

The church of St Mary of the Assumption was a grade II listed building, constructed in the late nineteenth century of heavy, buff coloured sandstone. Years of dedication and sheer effort had gone into its design and construction and its completed height, presence and overall grandeur gave it a gravitas worthy of a place built to worship Almighty God.

Blue slate tiles covered the steeply pitched roof and the windows were elongated, gothic arches with multi coloured stained glass biblical scenes. The high ceilings were criss crossed with arched vaulting. Everything about the structure was designed to focus the Victorian sinner's eyes heavenward.

Rose had closed her shop for the day, as a mark of respect for a valued customer and dear friend. She now waited patiently in an ornate pew surveying the beautiful interior of the Catholic church, named after the mother of Christ.

Traditional furnishings of polished hardwood, crisp, starched linen edged with embroidery and lace, gilded ornamentation and finely carved statuary were abdundantly evident in the old church.

The aromatic scents of wood polish, burning incense, candlewax and age hung intoxicatingly heavy in the air, evocative of times past.

DS Rasheed, as representative of the force, entered the church and quietly took a seat on the back pew, dressed in a smart, dark suit and a black tie in keeping with the solemnity of the occasion.

Family members and friends gradually filled the remaining pews. Their footsteps echoed with a scratchy, gritty sound on the stone floor due to the acoustics of the large space. This had the effect of causing people to whisper in hushed tones as they entered the nave.

The church called for reverence from those within its walls and so, Rose sat quietly, respectfully waiting for her dead friend.

Eventually, Greta arrived, making her grand entrance carried by four, strong men. She would have loved that, thought Rose, inwardly smiling. Then, feeling sadness, Rose mused that this was about the only part of the whole ceremony she would have enjoyed. Mr. and Mrs. Grey walked in melancholy procession behind their daughter, before taking their seats on the front pew, as the coffin was respectfully lowered onto a central stand.

She knew Greta would have hated every aspect of the whole funeral service, especially the church, but it was not Rose's place to pass comment.

Greta just wasn't into the whole Christian thing. Rejecting Rome and the papal religion all of her adult life, she followed a more nature driven lifestyle, the roots of which lay in belief systems that were followed by people centuries before Jesus Christ was even born. She would have despised the formality of the Catholic church service, much preferring a simpler celebration of her life, without pomp and ceremony.

Her grieving parents, however, would have nothing less than a full church burial service led by a sanctified priest for their only daughter.

They wanted the best for her, they always had, and as life long Roman Catholics, from a line of Roman Catholics that went as far back as the seventeenth century, they naturally wanted the rites and rituals that would send their daughter safely to heaven. Anything less was an anathema to their strongly held beliefs.

So Rose stayed respectfully silent. Hymns were sung, prayers were said, the body and blood of Christ were consumed and a touching eulogy was given. With a final hymn, Greta was carried out of the church, accompanied by the rich but doleful sound of the pipe organ, to the waiting hearse, waxed and buffed to a gleaming shine. It was a miserable day, in every sense of the word. The sky was a patchwork of grey clouds spitting a constant, fine drizzle over the town as the hearse began it's journey to the town cemetary, followed by a procession of cars. Slowly they wound their way through the town, like some slow moving, black, slithering snake until they reached the cemetery.

In the grounds, the final stage of Greta's last rite of passage began, the commital of her body to the earth.

At the graveside, the sodden mourners stood on the artificial grass; hands clasped, umbrellas up, heads down, listening to the words of the priest as he followed the prescribed script of the internment service.

Greta's mother stood quietly sobbing, her husband's arm protectively around her shoulders. Rose hadn't brought an umbrella and her pink hair hung in soggy tendrils covering her eyes. She silently offered up her own prayer to the Goddess as Greta's shiny, rosewood coffin was lowered into the damp earth.

Rose chose not to stay for the wake, which was to be held in the nearby Catholic club. Instead, she travelled back over the Lancashire moors, through the mist of fine drizzle, into Yorkshire and the Calder Valley. Windscreen wipers waving a melancholy rhythm until she arrived at her little cottage in Hebden Bridge.

The damp and cold seemed to have soaked into her very core. After towel drying her hair, Rose made herself a warming mug of tea and sat on the comfy, blue sofa. The cats seemed to sense her sadness and snuggled up next to her as she drank her brew, and remembered her friend in her own, deeply personal, way.

Chapter TwentyTwo. Grief.

Outside, the weather had turned suddenly wintry. A biting wind whipped across the Calder Valley, causing the temperatures to plummet in Hebden Bridge. Birds fluffed up their feathers to trap what little body heat they could and hedgehogs who were fattened enough, settled down to hibernate through the cold winter to come.

Rose sat on the squishy blue sofa, legs tucked underneath her and a multi coloured crochet blanket covering her from her shoulders to her toes. A fire was burning brightly in the log burner, but Rose still felt cold. Elemanzer was curled up on her lap and Akuba was tucked in the gap behind her knees. She was glad of the warmth coming from the two cats as she felt chilled to the bone.

Her laptop was open on the sofa arm and she was checking sales in her online shop. Or at least she was supposed to be, her head felt thick and slow. She was finding it difficult to concentrate.

Rose sighed. She just couldn't keep focused on her work. Smothered in a cold, she felt awful, despite the Olbas oil on her pyjama top and the vapour rub on her feet under her fluffy socks. She couldn't stop thinking about Greta Grey and her murder. It kept going round and around in her head. How one minute you could be full of life and energy and beauty, the next, dead. Greta had often stopped to chat in Rose's little shop. She was a lovely woman, clever, spiritual, giving. It was just horrible that this had happened to her friend. It was so sad.

She stroked Ellie's smooth coat, more to soothe herself than the cat. Giving up trying to work, Rose closed the laptop and put her head on the arm of the sofa for a nap, soon falling fast asleep.

She dreamt of Greta. Beautiful, vibrant, free spirited Greta, dancing naked around the bonfire with the others at the Samhain festival last October. Bodies twirling and twisting like the flames themselves. She could smell the cold of the night and the burning of the wood on the fire. Rose could hear the crackling sounds from the fire as it sparked and popped and the laughter that came from the freedom of the dance. The dancing became faster and wilder. The magic stronger.

Then she heard screams. High pitched, blood-curdling screams, as the fire began to consume the dancing women. The flames began licking at their feet, then rising higher, enveloping the whole of the dancers bodies in searing, blistering heat. The smell of burning flesh hung in the smokey air as their skin first reddened then began bubbling into great, glossy blisters that burst and sizzled in the flames. The screaming went on and on. A deafening, mournful, incessant wailing.

Rose tried to help but she couldn't. Something stopped her. She felt weak. Like she was stuck in glue. The women were burning, like the witches of old at the stake and Rose was powerless to help. She fought to get free, straining against invisible bonds and kicking out with her feet.

Then suddenly, she was awake, back on the blue sofa, Elemanzer slinking away in disgust as Rose's movements when dreaming had pushed him off her lap and onto the floor.

She was crying and sweating and shivering at the same time.

She felt so ill.

Closing her hot eyelids, Rose prayed to the Goddess for healing.

"Oh Great Goddess,
Mother of all,
By your healing powers,
Help your servant.
I pray for healing from the waters of Brigid's sacred well.
Restore me, O Goddess."

Rose then climbed the stairs to bed. She would be asleep before Yasmin came home, as would both cats, curled up with their mistress on the patchwork quilt.

Liam was sat up in his bed. A freezing wind was whistling over the Pennines and down into the valley where Burnley sprawled across the River Calder and the River Brun.

The gritters were out in force, making the roads safe for tomorrow's traffic, their yellow lights flashing as they sprayed salt liberally over both the tarmac and the last of the commuters as they made their weary way home.

Liam could feel a cold draught blowing through his bedroom from the open ventilation brick, but he wouldn't close it. He believed in the cleansing qualities of fresh air.

Instead, Liam pulled up the striped, flannelette sheet, and the itchy army blanket and drank a large, medicinal brandy that burned his throat and warmed his stomach.

Then, Liam closed his eyes and prayed.

"My Father, Almighty God.
One true Lord of all,
I give thanks for your never ending mercy,
Forgive your servant of his weaknesses,
Heal me Oh Lord.
Give your servant strength,
Equip me Oh Lord.
Let your will be done,
On this earth,
As it is in heaven,
Use your servant Lord,
I give myself willingly to your service,
Tell me your bidding and I will act,
All in the name and power of our Lord, Jesus Christ.
Amen. "

Then, Liam waited, keeping his eyes tightly shut, listening. Waiting patiently for God to answer his prayer.

He remembered his own dead father, Drago, saying to him, "No prayer goes unanswered. "

Liam believed in that promise with all his heart. He sat, his eyes closed, perfectly still, perfectly quiet, calmly and submissively waiting for the word of God. The wind howled outside, almost an inhuman sound. Liam listened. In those howls, Liam thought he heard a faint whisper. Did he imagine that?

He frowned and behind his closed eyes, he strained to see or to hear. Two minutes passed. Another whisper. This time he caught a word. Liam sat, motionless, keeping his breathing steady, waiting for any message, any communication.

Six minutes passed, then it happened again. Whispers in the wind. He listened intently and heard it. It became clearer. Easier to separate from the incessant whine of the wind. God began to whisper His will to Liam. He had looked down on His faithful servant with favour, and had spoken to him through the cold, northern wind.

Chapter TwentyThree. Shibden.

Yasmin had been worried about Rose following Greta's death. She seemed to be taking it very hard. Yasmin had noticed Rose smiled less and seemed sort of 'flat.' Yasmin decided they needed to get out into the fresh air and blow away the cobwebs.

They were well into autumn now and the day was cold but dry, so here they were at Shibden Hall, the family home of the infamous Anne Lister. They'd both loved the drama series, Gentleman Jack, and agreed that the actress who played Anne, Suranne Jones was so unbelievably hot in that role, despite the strange hairstyle!

They'd wrapped themselves up to keep warm, with woollen scarves, hats and gloves and sturdy boots for walking.

Getting out of the little car after the drive through West Yorkshire and into Halifax, they paid their entrance fee and began to explore. Anne Lister was mistress of Shibden Hall in the 19th century, but more importantly, was a lesbian in an era where such a thing was rarely spoken of. She wrote volume upon volume of diaries detailing every aspect of her life, the more salacious aspects written in secret code.

Yasmin and Rose strolled leisurely around the beautiful gardens. They toured Anne's home, walking the same corridors that Anne had walked in her trademark black attire, well over a century before. It felt strangely intrusive, as they knew so many private, intimate details of her life, but also very reverent as they admired this strong woman who lived her life on her own terms, a real pioneer of her time.

Stopping at the café for coffee and some delicious coffee and walnut cake, looking out over the lake, they held hands, feeling relaxed as they watched the mallard ducks and canada geese. It was a beautiful place, and they couldn't help but feel slightly envious of Anne owning all this acreage and living in her impressive, gothic home.

A motorised bright blue 'train' passed by carrying visitors and their children around the grounds.

"Do you ever want children?" asked Yasmin gazing wistfully at the laughing little faces riding the train.

"I never even thought I'd find love," said Rose, "It's amazing that in these 'enlightened' times I still feel set apart somehow."

"Rose," said Yasmin, looking her square in the face, "Never, ever doubt you are worthy of love. You are the kindest, most caring, funniest and sexiest woman I know."

Rose smiled, "I do love you, you know, and in answer to your question, children would be the icing on the cake, but in a year or two. I want you all to myself a bit longer yet."

"Sounds like a plan," said Yasmin, with a glitter in her eyes and a broad smile. They shared a kiss, each feeling love for the other. Gloved hand in gloved hand, they walked the woodland paths around the hall. Beautiful in their autumn finery, the trees were clothed in firey hues, and had carpeted the path with their colour; deep reds, warm russets, mellow ambers and bright yellows. Leaves crunching underfoot, they walked through the woods hearing the cooing sounds of wood pigeons, the twittering song of chaffinches and the noisy calls and wing flapping of crows. Squirrels dashed in short jerky sprints across their path and then disappeared up into the trees chattering as if annoyed by the human disturbance.

"It's beautiful this time of year," commented Rose.

Yasmin nodded, "I think we chose the best time of year to visit."

"I can picture Anne Lister walking through these woods hand in hand with Miss Walker, just as we are today," added Rose, "Safe from the judgemental stares of the townsfolk."

Yasmin nodded, "Maybe, by the generation after ours, same sex couples will be as unremarkable as heteros."

They passed a horse chestnut tree with it's large, yellow palmate leaves and spiky green fruits wrapped around their large, glossy seeds and stopped to collect handfuls of the deep brown, shiny conkers to take home as a deterrent to house spider invasion.

Stood on a knee height branch by the side of the path, they saw a robin, its feathers fluffed up against the cold and its scarlet breast on display. Rose took his picture on her phone.

After a good walk, Rose felt so much better, and as they climbed back into the car, she was twittering away almost as much as the chaffinches in the wood. Yasmin was happy to see a day outside had done Rose some good and was now feeling very hungry.

Yasmin and Rose stopped for an impromptu dinner at a lovely country pub they spotted on the way home, with rustic candlelit tables and a cosy, old fashioned feel. They chatted away as they ate mushroom risotto washed down with iced soda water, followed by a yummy tiramisu for Yasmin and a raspberry panacotta for Rose.

It had been a lovely day, and when they finally arrived home, the two women made slow, passionate love before falling into a deep, contented sleep in each others arms.

Chapter TwentyFour. Shopping.

Janet Brown and Darren Hewitt walked along the line of shops together with Janet's two children, three year old Harry and two year old Amy. Amy was in her pushchair whilst Harry walked between the couple, one small hand in Darren's and the other holding his mother's hand.

They'd been seeing each for over a month now, and Janet had decided it was time her children met Darren.

It was a Saturday and they were making their way up to the market hall. Harry ran to press the call button on the lift that would take up to the first floor level, where the market was situated. Once in the lift, Harry pushed the button to send it up. As the doors to the first floor opened, the little family spilled out and began to wander around the stalls. They looked at cheeses and cooked meats. Janet bought some potato pies for tea.

Suddenly, spotting the familiar, blue dolphin ride, Harry started pulling on the arms of the adults, excitedly drawing them towards it.

"Go on then," said Janet smiling, "You can have a turn."

The bright blue, painted dolphin had stood in the market hall in Burnley centre for as long as she could remember. Janet had ridden on its blue back when she was a child, as had her mum before her. It's paintwork was a little dated, it had been repainted numerous times, but it still worked perfectly. What made it even more special, and loved by money concious local families, was that the fare hadn't changed in decades. Now, as years ago, a two pence coin was all that was needed to ride the dolphin.

Harry went first, his mum posted a coin into the slot, which started the dolphin gently rocking backwards and forwards as though it were leaping the waves. Harry held on tight, grinning all the time and Janet took a picture of him on her phone.

Next, it was the turn of two year old Amy. Janet kept a protective hand at her daughter's back as she giggled with pleasure riding the dolphin. More photos were taken by Janet, wanting capture each happy moment and make memories.

"It's amazing how much fun you can have for 2p," said Darren, "I remember going on this as a kid."

"I bet most of the backsides in Burnley have sat on this dolphin," laughed Janet, "It's been here forever!"

When the ride stopped, Darren suggested they go for a coffee, so the group made their way to a café in the hall. The racket of the milk frother and the shouting of orders made the café a noisy place, but the coffee was always good and the cafe always busy.

Darren bought coffees for the adults, cartons of apple juice for the children and four slices of deliciously moist, homemade carrot cake. They found an empty table and ate their cakes, Harry and Amy scattering more crumbs over the formica surface than actually ended up in their mouths. The cream cheese frosting made their little cheeks and fingers so sticky and Janet had to find a couple of wet wipes to clean the two children after their food.

Neither Darren nor Janet minded the mess, they were just happy in each others company and enjoying spending time with the two children.

Later that evening, when the children were tucked up in bed, as Janet and Darren lay on her tan sofa, relaxed and happy, she scrolled through the pictures she had taken and uploaded the best ones to Facebook. She then changed her status to 'in a relationship.'

Janet had finally decided that Darren could stay overnight. She wouldn't agree to him staying over for the full night earlier in their relationship as it was too new and she had explained that she didn't want her children waking up to a stranger in their mother's bed. Darren respected that. He admired her strength and the love and consideration she showed for her children. In fact, he felt he might be falling a little in love with them himself. They were the cutest kids, and he enjoyed being involved in a little, ready made family.

Getting up off the sofa, Darren took Janet gently by the hand, and smiling, led her to bed.

Liam was at home and already in his bed. A single divan with sheets and traditional blankets. He didn't like duvets, he preferred the weighty feeling a blanket gave.

Scrolling through the Facebook posts on his phone, Liam suddenly stopped. Frowning, he studied the photo of a grinning Darren and

Janet looking out of the small screen. He tapped on the photo, then used his thumb and finger to make it larger. There it was.

"More proof," he murmured to himself, shaking his head. Liam sighed. He had tried to warn her.

Getting out of his bed, Liam dropped to his knees and began to pray.

Chapter TwentyFive. Autopsy.

The sky was a beautiful, cerulean blue sparsely scattered with fluffy white clouds. Sunshine kept the autumn temperature to a pleasant 11°C. Not bad for a September day in Lancashire. It was a good day to be alive thought Mr. Monroe as he parked his volvo in the staff carpark. Perhaps he would call Geoffery for a round of golf this afternoon, he mused, as he walked into the hospital mortuary.

The Insect-o-cuter buzzed as another blue bottle, attracted by the scent of decomposition, was lured in by the UV tubes to be zapped by the live metal grid.

The body of Greta Grey lay on the steel autopsy table, her head raised on a block and her damp hair combed off her face. It didn't look like Greta. Even her own mother had difficulty identifying her daughter.

It's amazing how quickly the familiar and loved can degenerate into something abhorrent and repugnant. How instead of hugs and kisses, we back away and wrinkle our noses. How we stop referring to them by their given name, but rather use impersonal terms such as 'the body,' 'the deceased,' or 'the corpse.' Even less respectful were terms such as 'carrion,' for that is what Greta Grey had become. Carrion, for the crows, the flies, the rats, the foxes. Nature wastes nothing. Nature is the perfect recycler. Simplifying our parts to feed the earth once more.

He had advised Mrs Grey that the body of her daughter could be identified without a viewing but the mother had been insistent. He honestly hoped her memories of her daughter would be of her in life, rather than as she was now.

After the pathologist's initial inspection of the clothed body, his assistant had carefully removed her clothing, bagging, sealing and labelling each item to preserve the chain of evidence. He bagged her silver trace chain necklace and her moonstone ring, which had helped with identification. These would be returned to her family, thoroughly cleaned, if and when the investigation concluded.

He then began removing the maggots, preserving a few to process as specimens. The life cycles of the various insect species were extremely accurate in identifying the length of time the body had been left exposed in this type of situation. It was important to note climatic conditions and temperatures in conjunction with the specimens. Some would be boiled and then preserved in 50% Isopropyl alcohol. Others would be kept to maturity to determine identity.

An artist's paintbrush was then dipped in water to remove insect egg samples from both facial and genital orifices.

His assistant had then washed the body with mild detergent and water. The fetid smell of decomposition still hung heavily in the room, and James Monroe, the forensic pathologist, wiped vapour rub under his nostrils to partially mask the scent. He knew that the smell could not be totally eradicated and would linger both in the room and on his own clothing.

He carefully removed the polythene bags that had been secured with elastic bands around the hands and took scrapings from underneath each manicured nail, preserving any debris found in plastic tubes. The blood that had dried on her fingers he found to be bite marks from rodents, probably rats.

He spoke into a handheld recorder, noting his findings as he worked. He took photographs of the bruising around Greta's neck. Rolling the body with the help of his assistant, he noted that she had a small star shaped tattoo on the nape of her neck and photographed it.

His assistant had previously retracted the ribs with bone cutters that were, in principle, very like the cutters used on small to medium tree branches. This would expose the organs, which he now removed, one at a time, weighing them and disecting them in narrow slices to determine if any abnormality, disease or injury was apparent. He found a tampon present in Greta's vagina and noted menses which would have attracted both insect and mammalian scavengers.

Finally the brain. His assistant had separated the skull cap using a bone saw above the eyebrows. The scalp was separated from the bone and retracted over the face. Mr Monroe lifted the skull cap off with a squelch, removed the brain b y separating the optic nerve and spinal cord connections before placing it on the bench. The brain was severely decomposed and beginning to liquify. He looked for signs of hemorrhage or damage, finding bruising to the rear of the brain. He again used his knife to slice the brain into thin sections to assess for deeper damage or disease. The brain is a delicate organ and the slices almost melted as he worked due to microbial activity breaking down the structure of the brain.

Mr Monroe recorded all his findings to be typed up later into a formal report, copies of which would be sent to both the police investigatory lead and the coroner.

Removing his gloves and apron, Monroe left Greta, or what used to be Greta, a daughter, a successful solicitor, an attractive young woman. Now, ceased to be Greta, deceased, dead, the body, in the care of his assistant who would restore the organs to the corpse and clean the equipment.

James Monroe then returned to his office and washed his hands before taking his sandwich box from the fridge and boiling the kettle to make himself a mug of tea.

Chapter TwentySix.
Investigation.

DI Johnson had read through the PM report and was discussing the results with DS Abdul Rasheed.

"So, no sign of sexual assault. She was found fully clothed. Death by asphyxiation from manual strangulation."

"Was she killed at the scene?" asked Rasheed.

"It would appear not. There were still traces of the pattern of lividity present that suggested she was in a foetal position for some time before she was dumped. We found her car abandoned outside the gym she used. So maybe transported in another car or something?"

Rasheed thought about that. Gravity meant the blood pooled after death, sinking to the parts of the body nearest the ground. The woman had been found lying on her back, but the purple lividity pattern was right sided, with blanching where limbs were bent. It did seem likely the murder site wasn't where the body was found.

PC Sarah Preston was making tea in the staff room of the police station.

"Johnson, one sugar, Rasheed, two sweetners" she muttered to herself before adding milk and stirring the mugs.

Carrying one mug in each hand, she opened the door with a nudge of her hip and carried them into DI Ian Johnson's office.

"Thanks Sarah," said the DI before he picked up his mug and took a tentative sip.

"Ooo, just what the doctor ordered, thanks Sarah, you're a star," added DS Rasheed. PC Preston smiled, closed the office door behind her leaving the two superior officers to their meeting and went back to typing up a burglary report at her desk.

DS Abdul Rasheed left his tea to cool for a few moments and read from his notes as he spoke, "So, she's been identified from a bank card in her bag as Greta Grey. Also in her bag, thirty pounds in cash.

Ms. Grey was twenty eight years old, single. Next of kin, her parents, have been informed. They can't think of anyone who would want to hurt her..."

"No spurned boyfriend?" interjected DI Johnson.

"Nope," replied Rasheed, "Apparently, she's been single for over a year. Real career woman by all accounts."

"What career was that?" asked the DI.

"Law," replied the DS, "She'd studied for a law degree and had worked her way up to partner at Higson and Preston solicitors."

"Our paths had crossed before," Johnson recalled, "Grey, I remember her, very pretty and a damn good solicitor. Very professional. Such a shame. She would have had a good future ahead of her."

Abdul nodded in agreement, a real waste, as indeed were all lives cut short. This job taught you to never take tomorrow for granted, but to be kind whenever the opportunity arose. He looked at his notes again and continued,

" She was last seen on Friday evening at her gym on St. Peters Street, but didn't turn up for work after the weekend. She was wearing gym clothing when found, so it's highly likely death occurred on Friday night/Saturday morning."

"And she was found yesterday, Wednesday," said Johnson thoughfully, "So around five days before she was found, and nobody missed her?"

"Her mother said she tended to phone around once a fortnight and they'd last spoken on the seventeenth, so she wasn't expecting another call for maybe another week. Work said it was most unusual for her not to phone in if she was going to be off, but she was off Monday anyway so she wasn't missed until Tuesday. They'd attempted to call her but her phone was switched off. Her secretary called round on Wednesday evening, but found the house in darkness and no answer. After reading that we'd found a body, they called the station."

Ian Johnson frowned. This was a real puzzle. No sign of sexual assault, no robbery. What was the motive? A disgruntled client? Abdul Rasheed was equally bemused. Was this just a random attack? Doubtful. Strangulation was an emotional kind of killing.

" She had a contusion on the back of her head, right?" said Abdul, "So she was probably knocked out from behind, or at least, knocked to the ground, prior to strangulation."

Ian nodded, "Yes, that sounds probable. Unless she fell backwards and hit her head?"

They both sat, deep in thought. This one certainly wasn't straight forward.

PC Sarah Preston had taken her own mug of tea to her desk and after the burglary report, was now typing up statements from the boys who discovered the decomposing body of Greta Grey.

'I noticed a strange smell and flies buzzing around near a mattress. Toby and I lifted the mattress up then saw her lying on the ground. I thought her mouth was moving, but it was the maggots moving. I screamed. We dropped the mattress and ran away. Then…' she typed quickly, her long nails tip tapping away at the keys. Every few minutes, she took a sip of her tea, before continuing to type the statements.

By twelve o' clock, her stomach was growling.

'I declare, to the best of my knowledge and recollection, that this is a true and honest account.'

Sarah Preston saved her work on the computer before heading off to the staff canteen for lunch.

Chapter TwentySeven. Fifty.

Ian heard a gentle knock.

"Sir? The chief wants to see you asap," Sarah Preston said as she popped her head around Ian's office door.

Ian sighed, he was just about to make a move home. Putting down his pen on the cluttered desk top, he reluctantly stood up, "On my way," he answered wearily.

Ian walked down the blue carpeted corridor to the Chief Inspector's spacious office.

Knocking on the dark wood effect door, he waited for the usual,"Enter," before opening it.

"Happy Birthday!" shouted his whole team in unison with the accompanying streamers from half a dozen party poppers.

"You didn't think we'd let your fiftieth go by without some fanfare, did you Ian?" said Chief Inspector Ruth Emmerson, smiling broadly and handing him a glass of sparkling white wine.

It wasn't Ian's actual birthday until Sunday, but that was his day off so the little celebration was brought forward.

" I was hoping it would slip under the radar" he replied laughing, "I'm getting far too many candles on the cake for my liking!"

"Nonsense!" said the grinning Chief, "Plenty of life in the old dog yet."

"Happy fiftieth, Sir!" said a smiling Sarah Preston as she clinked her glass on his own, "Sorry about the ruse."

Ian smiled, "You're forgiven," he replied in good humour.

Ishmael Patel shouted out a cheesy, "You don't look a day over forty nine, Sir!" to which Ian replied, "Cheeky sod," with a grin.

Music started up from someone's phone connected to a small speaker and bowls of twiglets and cheese balls were passed around.

Quite a few of the younger members of the team had left their cars at home or organised lifts, as they were hoping to make a night of it so the Prosecco flowed freely. It felt good to let their hair down and it helped cement their relationships as a team. Ian stuck to the one glass. He was driving and, more importantly, he wanted to be home with Eve at a reasonable hour.

John Carpenter, Jakub Kowalski, Abdul Rasheed, Jagpal Randhawa, Adam White, Ibrahim Choudary and Sarah Preston all decided to go for an Indian in town. They'd brought their 'civvie' clothes, so a quick change and for the women, a touch of lipstick, and they were ready to go. Piling into two cars, driven by, Abdul and Ibrahim, they soon arrived at the small car park outside the restaurant.

Carved stone lions flanked the entrance to the restaurant as the group went inside.

Impressive chandeliers hung from the ceilings and banquettes of gold, crushed velvet gave the award winning restaurant a luxurious feeling of opulence. As soon as they walked through the doors, tempting aromas of garlic and spices from the restaurant kitchen, made them hungry. Adam had brought a couple of the bottles of prosecco as the restaurant had a 'bring your own alcohol' policy, and set about opening the first as soon as the group were seated. The non-drinkers ordered their juice and cola and the group studied the extensive menu.

After a good couple of hours of delicious, spicy dishes, giant naan breads and lots of laughter, the team left the restaurant.

Abdul, John and Ibrahim said their goodbyes and set off home. The remaining members of the group decided that the night was yet young and it was time to find a club.

The music was loud. Too loud to hear each other speak, but all three officers still going strong, were quite merry by now and were doing more dancing than talking.

Adam was really going for it on the dancefloor and Jakub was taking the mick out of him mercilessly with the two women. Jagpal and Sarah then began throwing some shapes of their own as Jakub went to the bar for a double vodka. All four were enjoying the chance of some downtime from their stressful work lives.

By two in the morning, they were ready to call it a day and stumbled drunkenly into the cold night air to find a cab.

In the cab, the four workmates were still chatting away as they drew up outside Jagpal's house.

"Don't wake up that husband of yours," said Adam in a stage whisper, with a forefinger against his lips.

"See you Monday," replied Jagpal, far more soberly than her younger colleague, who had drank more than his fair share of the prosecco.

The cab stopped outside the old church building that now contained six flats, one of which was home to Sarah Preston.

"Not going to invite me in?" ventured Adam hopefully, slurring his words.

"Not a chance," laughed Sarah, shutting the cab door on her drunken friends. As the cab drove away, Adam pulled a mock sad face at the window.

Bursting into laughter again, Sarah fished in her bag for her keys.

"Hello," said a male voice, making Sarah jump.

She swiftly turned, her startled face turning to a smiling one, "You didn't half give me a scare!" she said with a nervous giggle.

"I'm so sorry, my bad," the good-looking man answered apologetically, "You're flat six aren't you?"

"Yes, I'm Sarah," she replied with an outstretched hand.

"I'm Chris, flat three," he said, taking her hand and shaking it, "Let me get the door for you."

Chris held open the door for her and then followed her in.

"Well, goodnight Chris," said Sarah as she started up the stairs.

"Night, see you later, Sarah," Chris replied.

As Sarah locked the door of her flat and took off her jacket, she smiled to herself. She had a feeling she might be seeing more of Chris.

Chapter TwentyEight. Hungover.

Sarah woke up with a headache. She was getting too old for this clubbing malarkey, she thought to herself as she winced and squinted her way to the bathroom for paracetamol. Swallowing two of the white tablets with a gulp of water, straight from the tap, she groaned loudly as she caught a glimpse of her reflection in the bathroom mirror. Mascara was smudged under both of her green eyes which were decidedly bloodshot. Her hair was tangled and stuck up and she had a yellow pimple on her chin. Squeezing the offending blemish left two half moons in her skin and an angry red spot.

Her mouth was dry and rough, so she walked slowly to the kitchen and put the kettle on to boil. Sitting down at the breakfast bar with her head in her hands, Sarah waited. Hearing the click of the kettle, she threw a teabag into a mug and poured the boiling water on top. Opening the door of the fridge, Sarah saw she was low on milk, but there was just about enough for one brew.

Tea made, she went into the living room and sat on the black leather sofa. Holding the mug in both hands, she sipped the hot tea. It was good. The paracetamol were beginning to work, her head was feeling a little better. Sarah clicked the tv remote and found a weekend cooking show. She sipped her tea and watched the show's host make a forest fruit crumble.

By the time he'd poured on the custard, she felt a lot better. Well enough to think about going to the shop for some milk.

After a quick shower, which helped clear her head and rid her of the stale smells of the night before, she dressed for comfort rather than style, in a baggy t-shirt, joggers and a sweat top. Adding a peaked cap to hide her hair, she headed out to the local convenience store. The day was cold and fresh. Just the kind of weather needed to blow away the cobwebs with a brisk walk.

It wasn't far to the shop, maybe ten minutes or so, and Sarah was enjoying the feeling of fresh air on her skin after too many hours indoors. She passed teenagers practising bike tricks and a young mum with a pushchair heading towards town. Catching a glimpse of the child, mainly hidden from view by his woolly hat and zipped up coat, she wondered when she would have a child. She was twenty four now and very single. Whilst not exactly feeling as though time were running out, she was at that age where she was curious as to what the future would bring.

Opening the door to the shop, she beamed a cheery hello to the shopkeeper before getting a pint of milk out of a tall fridge and taking it to the counter. Falling for the old impulse buy trick, she grabbed a bar of chocolate from the tray that was strategically placed to optimise add on purchases.

Sarah paid for her milk and chocolate, thanked the middle aged woman behind the till and turned to leave, almost bumping into Chris from flat three entering the shop.

"Hello again," he said, flashing a smile that showed off his very good teeth.

"Hello," answered Sarah, wishing she'd put a bit if make up on before she'd left her flat. Embarrassed, she kept her head down and quickly left the cramped shop.

Typical, she thought to herself, as she walked home. The one day I go out sans make up and with hardly a brush through my hair, I bump into a nice looking man.

"Sarah!" she heard someone call her name. Turning around, she noticed Chris, swinging a loaf of bread in one hand, jogging to catch up with her.

Now feeling mortified at her appearance, she became shy and stuck for conversation. Chris had no such trouble and was soon chatting away like he'd known her for donkey's years. Her shyness gradually evaporated and she began laughing and joking with him as they walked. They talked about tv and films and found they both loved a good horror movie.

On reaching their flats, Chris casually mentioned that there was a new Joker movie showing at the cinema next week that he really wanted to see and he wondered if they should go together. Sarah said she would, and that they would work out the details later in the week, giving him her mobile number. They said their goodbyes and Sarah smiled to herself as she climbed her stairs.

Chapter TwentyNine. Chris.

Chris let himself into his flat, swinging the bread onto the counter top. He whistled to himself happily as he took margarine and sliced ham out of the fridge, and a side plate out of one of the white gloss wall cupboards and made himself a sandwich. After pouring a glass of milk, he took both over to the pale grey, fabric sofa, setting them down on the white gloss coffee table.

As he ate, he thought about Sarah Preston. He liked her. She was funny and smart. Before he went out that morning, he was already looking forward to the new Joker movie, now he was looking forward to it even more. He'd been single now for about five months after a long term relationship had run its natural course.

Chris Jameson was twenty nine years old and worked as a software developer. He was very into his technology and was always on the lookout for the next gadget. Serious about his gaming, he spent hours killing zombies and soldiers of various nationalities at the weekends, excusing it as 'research.'

With his blond hair and brown eyes, he never had a problem attracting the ladies and exuded a natural confidence that they found hard to resist.

Another passion of his was motorbikes. His pride and joy was a Triumph Bonneville T120, with its iconic styling and finished in a matt black. He loved that bike. The classic lines, the smooth curves, the Triumph engine and chrome exhaust. It was a beautiful machine.

He'd aspired towards owning one for ages and saved hard to get it. Riding around the country lanes on a sunny weekend afternoon gave him such a feeling of freedom. He hoped Sarah liked to ride pillion.

Sarah put the milk on the worktop and filled the kettle. Getting a mug from the wall cupboard, she threw in a teabag and half a teaspoon of sugar. She didn't usually take sugar in her tea, but a hangover day called for a little sweetness.

As the kettle boiled she thought about Chris. He really did seem perfect. Good looking, good job, good sense of humour and living, quite literally, right on her doorstep. Too good to be true she questioned herself, with a touch of cynicism.

The kettle switched itself off with a click and Sarah poured the boiling water into her mug, shaking any negative thoughts out of her head.

Taking her tea to the sofa, along with the chocolate, Sarah sat down and thought about her date. It was months since she'd last been to see a movie at the cinema. She'd watched 'Bohemian Rhapsody,' an biograpical film about Freddie Mercury with her Queen mad friend Lou. Now that was a good film, she thought. Freddie Mercury was one of a kind and the world had lost him far too soon.

Now, what should she wear? It was the cinema so definitely casual. Jeans and a nice top. She broke off a square of chocolate and popped it in her mouth as she pondered.

She'd not long bought a bright red, oversized shirt with tiny flowers all over the fabric. That would be comfortable and look good for a first date she thought.

She took a sip of her tea. Jeans, red shirt and maybe some gold hoop earrings and her brown suede boots. There, outfit sorted!

She clicked the remote for the tv. Netflix. She'd been wanting to watch Birdbox for ages now, but never found the time. Deciding that today was, most decidedly, a lazy day, she settled down to watch the film, eating her chocolate and drinking her tea.

Downstairs, in flat three, Chris was sat on his sofa, playing on the Ps4, killing enemy soldiers with his squad. He was miked up and his earphones were on.

"Come on lads! Enemy to the east," he called out, encouraging his fellow soldiers onwards. Manoevering through the rubble of a bombed out landscape, he barked instructions to his teammates. Totally lost in the virtual world, he led his soldiers into battle, adrenalin pumping, weapons ready.

They were almost at the target, they'd wiped out a good number of enemy insurgents already and were making swift progress.

Peering around the corner of a ruined house, he picked off a couple more as he circled behind them and saw them crouched behind their weapons. Leaving their dead corpses on the sand he ran forward, leading his band of brothers to an almost cerain victory.

Over a ridge, "Fuck!" They were surprised by a further pocket of resistance but fought well and soon more dead bodies of the enemy littered the ground.

Moving ever onward, Chris stopped to reload, before shouting, "Fire in the hold," and throwing a virtual grenade into an occupied house, blowing enemy soldiers to smithereens. The house was clear and…red filled the screen, he was shot dead. not just shot dead, shot dead by friendly fire.

"Fucking retard! What did you do that for you daft cunt?" he spat venemously into the mike, not caring if his opponent were nine or nineteen, before ripping off his headphones and kicking over his coffee table.

Chris got up, still furious and got a beer from the fridge, ripping the tab off the can, sending splashes of lager onto the floor. He took a few good gulps from the can before righting the coffee table, and giving himself a few minutes to calm down. With a determined sigh, he sat upright, put his headphones back on and spoke into the mike,

"Right. Come on you fuckers. Get your shit together and let's do this!"

Chapter Thirty. Suspicion.

They'd been called out on a missing persons call. It was a mild, autumnal day, with a slight breeze that didn't quite have enough strength to blow the first of the yellow leaves from the silver birch tree in the garden of Cheryl's bungalow.

Cheryl's sister had phoned the police after not being able to contact her for over a week. They usually phoned or messaged each other every two or three days and Susan had become concerned when Cheryl's phone appeared to have been switched off every time she had tried to contact her. Having moved to Lincolnshire several years ago with her husband, she couldn't just 'pop round' to check on Cheryl, but the sisters were still close and kept in regular contact. Susan had even tried phoning the office of the firm Cheryl worked for and they told Susan that Cheryl was off sick with a bad ear infection. That satisfied her for a few days, but even if she was ill, Susan knew that Cheryl would do her best to answer her messages. She was getting increasingly worried as the days passed by. She was probably over reacting, she thought, and there would be a perfectly simple explanation, but she felt she had to phone the police just for her own peace of mind.

PC Sarah Preston was shading her eyes and peering into the front window of the house.

"Her car's still here," said PC Adam White, "Maybe she had a friend come and pick her up if she was feeling so ill?" he suggested.

"Maybe," said Sarah, unconvinced, moving to the bedroom window. Through the windows, everything looked in its place. She'd seen the tidy hallway and the front of the L-shaped through lounge which looked immaculate. In the bedroom, the bed was made and all looked as it should be.

"I'm going to have a look around the back," she said to Adam as she opened the white painted, ornamental, wrought iron side gate and walked down the path to the rear of the house.

The lounge had lovely large patio doors onto the back garden and Sarah shaded her eyes with a flattened hand and looked inside. Fairly similar to what she'd seen from the front, but then she noticed it.

In the corner, near the patio door, was a dried up pile of dog mess. Sarah frowned. Cheryl Hargraves did not seem like the kind of woman who would allow her dog to mess in the house and just leave it on her lovely cream wool carpet.

Looking more closely, she saw yellowed patches of what looked like urine and more, fresher looking dog mess at the other side of the patio doors.

Sarah thought for a moment. There was no sign of the dog, no barking as they knocked in the door. If Cheryl had gone away, she would have taken her dog, but would she have left the mess in an otherwise spotless house? Something wasn't right. She radioed in, reporting the findings and asking advice.

"Adam," she called, "Can you check the neighbours. See if they've got a spare key? "

"Ok," Adam said and went to enquire next door.

Sarah had a quick look under the well kept plant pots but no spare keys were hidden there. She didn't see Cheryl as the type to leave keys around anyway, living alone as she did. Sarah walked back around to the front door.

Adam returned, looking pleased with himself, jangling a silver key on a fluffy, pink key ring.

He unlocked the front door and entered Cheryl's home. It felt cosy and warm. The heating was on a timer and had been switching on and off automatically. Cheryl would have altered the thermostat if she was going away, thought PC Preston.

They walked slowly through the hall, lots of unopened mail on the doormat, and then into the lounge. They could smell the dog mess now. There were numerous piles of it, and there, in a corner, behind a pink fabric armchair, lay a dead, black and white, pomeranian.

"Looks like it might have starved to death," said Adam sadly, he was a dog owner himself. Walking into the kitchen, Sarah saw the empty water bowl, "Dehydration kills faster," she said flatly.

It was an upsetting scene, but still didn't answer the question that was the purpose of their visit.

Where was Cheryl Hargraves?

PC White called in to the station. DS Rasheed would attend and they were to wait there until he arrived.

They used the time to check the dates on the mail in the hallway and look for any other clues to the mystery. They found Cheryl's spare car key in her bedroom drawer just as DS Rasheed pulled up behind Cheryl's Renault.

PC Preston met the DS outside and gave him the car key which he used to open the little, purple car.

"How tall was Ms. Hargraves, do we know?" he asked.

"Er… Missper report says five foot two, Sir," answered PC Preston.

"In that case," said DS Rasheed, "It looks like someone else last drove her car. The seat is pushed way back. She wouldn't have been able to reach the pedals. Could be significant."

He then entered the house where PC White showed him the dead dog.

"We'll get a vet to do a PM on the dog," the DS told the two PC's, "It might help us build a timeline. "

Sarah listened and watched intently as the older DS went about his investigation. Making mental notes and soaking up his experience of examining evidence, she was learning all the time and hoped to be involved in detective work herself one day.

Chapter ThirtyOne. Poppet.

Poppet lay on the veterinary table. The veterinary surgeon, Malcolm Davies, shaved the abdomen of the little pomeranian, the blades catching on the raised ribcage as he did so.

He picked up his scalpel and sliced into the dog to locate the stomach. As he suspected, the stomach was virtually empty, as was the majority of the intestine. It had been a number of days since the little dog had eaten anything.

Abdul Rasheed began to read,
NECROPSY REPORT
Date: 09/10/19
Veterinarian: Malcolm Davies
Carcass is that of a six year old, castrated male, microchipped, black and white Pomeranian dog in very poor nutrition.
GROSS FINDINGS
Weight: 1.15kg
Body as a whole: Emaciated, anaemia
GROSS DIAGNOSIS
Emaciation and dehydration
Note, dog left without food or water for an unknown number of days (minimum 3)

He stopped reading. So the dog had been without food and water for a minimum of three days. Abdul frowned. His gut told him that Cheryl Hargraves would never in a million years have voluntarily left her dog like that. So where was she?
Someone else had last driven her car, more than likely a male, due to leg length.
This wasn't going to end well. He was sure about that.

Chapter ThirtyTwo. Missing.

"Cheryl is missing?" said Janet incredulously, "What do you mean missing? I thought she had an ear infection?"

Mohammed had called the warehouse staff together to talk about Cheryl's disappearance.

"That's what we were told, but her sister has called the police because she was worried, and they've found her little dog, dead in her house," Mohammed said seriously, "Apparently, her car is there, but no sign of Cheryl. No one seems to know where she is. Its like she's just vanished."

The warehouse workers all looked expectantly at Mohammed, with confused frowns and worried looks.

"Do they have any idea where she could be?" asked Tariq with genuine concern.

"Maybe she just decided to go away for a while?" ventured Liam.

"No," said Janet adamantly, "She would never have left Poppet. She loved that little dog as if he were her baby."

Mohammed nodded in agreement .

"So do they think something has happened to her?" said Darren, voicing what none of the others had dared. Janet brought a hand to her mouth.

"I'm not saying that, I really don't know where she is or why she went. The police don't know either, but they might want to speak with us, to see if we know or heard anything," Mohammed told his team, "So have a think. Did Cheryl mention a trip or anything that might help the police find her."

They all nodded, silently trying to remember when they last saw her.

"I've been given some 'Missing' posters, so feel free to take as many as you want to put up around your local area. There are plenty and I can always get some more photocopied if needed," Mohammed handed out a number of posters to each raised hand.

"Thank you. Now I'm going to give you all a half hour break as it's a lot to take in," Mohammed said, "So go, grab a coffee, have a fag or whatever and I'll see you back at work in half an hour."

Darren went for a smoke, telling Janet he would meet her in the staffroom in five. Liam went after Darren. Janet, Tariq and Mohammed went to make their drinks.

"Poor Cheryl, I hope she's ok," said Janet sadly as she put the kettle on to boil, "And poor little Poppet."

Outside, Darren lit a cigarette and offered his disposable lighter to Liam, who took it and lit his own. Darren took a long drag on his cigarette, holding it in his lungs a moment before blowing out a thin stream of smoke. If things were different, Cheryl would have been with them, smoking her menthol cigarettes, but she was gone.

Fat raindrops from a recent shower, dripped lazily from gulleys in the corrugated roof of the designated smoking area. Darren could see his monochrome refection in the large puddle that had formed immediately in front of the dry area of tarmac as he leaned against a timber post, holding up the roof. He rocked the toe of his boot in the browny grey water, making concentric ripples move over the puddles surface that distorted his image.

Without turning his head Liam asked, "Do you think she went away, Darren," and then let the remaining smoke in his lungs escape slowly through his teeth and nostrils.

Liam kept his eyes on the horizon as he waited for Darren's answer. Darren thought for a moment before shaking his head, answering, "I don't know Liam. I just don't know."

Liam nodded and sighed, then frowning, drew on his cigarette hard, making the orange tip eat through the cigarette paper with a quiet crackling sound.

Darren seemed lost in thought and the two men smoked in silence before going inside to the staff room.

As they entered, they heard Mohammed speaking, "I really do hope they find her soon, In sh'Allah. She will be in my families prayers." Darren made himself a brew. Liam just had water. They all sat around the one table with their cold drinks and mugs of tea.

"Did she say anything about going away?" asked Mohammed to the group.

They all shook their heads.

"Can you think of anything she said in the days before she was off sick?" asked Janet to nobody in particular, "There must be something! I remember going in to the office with your card Liam.

When you lost your mother. She signed the card but didn't mention going away anywhere."

"She was gone when I returned to work," said Liam, "She had an ear infection."

"I last saw her when I went to the office to collect orders," added Mohammed, "She didn't mention anything to me."

"Would an ear infection affect your mind?" suggested Darren, "Like maybe she wandered off or something?"

"Maybe," nodded Liam in agreement.

Janet frowned. She wasn't so sure.

They all agreed to put the posters up on the lampposts and in the corner shop windows near to where each of them lived. It was all they could do. It wasn't much, but it was something. Cheryl, despite her faults was a friend, and her confusing and mysterious disappearance had unsettled and hurt them.

The rest of the day passed without joking around or flirty banter. It didn't feel right, knowing that Cheryl wasn't tapping away at the keyboard in the office, but somewhere else, maybe hurt or in trouble, or even something worse. The warehouse held a solemn air. One of its own were missing and they all felt the loss keenly.

Chapter ThirtyThree. Joker.

She was just adding the finishing touch to her make up, a slick of cherry lip gloss over the soft red lipstick. Sarah pulled on her jeans. The zip was a little more resistant than it used to be as Sarah was due to come on her period and she often felt bloated around that time of the month. She was annoyed with herself, but grateful she could still wear them. She slipped the oversized, bright red shirt over her head, taking care not to catch her lipgloss, and fastened the top buttons. The material was soft and flowing, meaning it draped really well. Printed onto the fabric were hundreds of tiny black and white flowers with mid green leaves giving it a soft, feminine feel.

She brushed through her glossy, almost black hair, smoothing it with a couple of drops of serum and found some large gold coloured hoops in her jewellery box and fastened them in her ears.

Lastly, she pulled on her nutmeg brown, suede boots and grabbed the beige suede biker jacket from the coat hooks by the door. Bag, keys, card, gloss, she said to herself, going through her mental checklist of items to remember before she locked up her flat and went downstairs to Chris' flat.

He was just locking his own door as she reached the bottom of the stairs.

"You look good," he said, as his eyes lowered then rose, appraising her whole look.

She caught the scent of some kind of delicious masculine fragrance, inhaling deeply to maximise the experience.

"Cab should be here any minute," he informed her as they walked outside their building.

Chris wore black jeans, with a pale grey 'All Saints' shirt, and brown lace up brogue style shoes.

The taxi rolled around the corner, coming to a stop outside the old church. Getting inside, they took the short journey through the town, towards the cinema, chatting easily throughout. They were both looking forward to the movie after hearing good reviews about Joaquin Phoenix's role as the mad and extremely bad, Joker.

The movie did not disappoint and they were both talking animatedly about it as they left the cinema and entered the pub opposite. "He played that role just right," said Chris as they reached the bar.

"Yes, and it must have been daunting having to follow Heath Ledger," said Sarah.

"Too right," Chris answered, "A bottle of malbec and two glasses please mate," he called to the bartender, "playing a role like that after Heath Ledger's death would be scary for an actor. Death kinda immortalises them in the role and it gets a harder act to follow."

Chris paid for the wine and they found a quiet table in a corner.

"I liked Jack Nicholson's Joker," said Sarah, "He brought that 'Here's Johnny' kind of madness from The Shining to it."

"It's a great character to play," Chris said, "A real tortured soul."

They talked happily as they drank their wine, enjoying each others company, until last orders were called and Chris phoned for a cab. The wine had made them both a little giddy and they were laughing at something and nothing as the taxi drew up to the kerb and they got in.

The cab drove the couple the short distance home and they got out just as the rain began to fall.

"Perfect timing!" said Chris as they entered the building and saw a flash of lightning and the rain begin to pour as they watched through the glass door.

He looked at Sarah and pulled her towards him, kissing her long and hard on the lips. She responded in kind, winding her arms around his neck and passionately kissing him back. He stepped back and took her hand to lead her to his flat.

"No, no, no," laughed Sarah, never on a first date, remembering her period.

Chris' expression changed to stone, "Are you serious?" he said in surprise.

Sarah felt suddenly uncomfortable. Her smile disappeared and she tried to explain, "I don't really know you well enough…"

"Fucking pricktease!" Chris spat, totally unused to not getting what he wanted, "Take my money then pie me off?" He looked at her in disgust.

Sarah turned on her heel and stormed angrily up the stairs. Slamming her front door shut behind her she found she was shaking with frustration.

"What a mysoginistic, self centred prick!" she shouted to the wall, feeling angry tears pricking at the corner of her eyes. She stamped her foot in annoyance that she hadn't come up with some slick oneliner to knock the wind out of that arrogant twats sails.

Throwing down her bag and jacket, she got straight on her phone to moan to her friend Maisie.

"I have just this minute come back from the worse date of my life," began Sarah and recounted the whole sorry tale to her friend, listening patiently on the other end of the line.

"What an absolute tool," commiserated Maisie on the phone to Sarah after she'd finally finished offloading, "Well, there's a new moon next Saturday," Maisie said pointedly.

"Is there?" said Sarah, suddenly feeling more positive, "Well, if that's not a blessing I don't know what is," she laughed.

"I was actually joking. Be careful," warned Maisie, "Remember the three fold rule."

"Don't worry," Sarah reassured her friend, "I'm only returning to him what he gave me."

"Ok. I personally don't think he's worth a second thought and you'd be better off just leaving him to the universe," said Maisie, "But it's your funeral."

"I think it's justice," said Sarah, anger and a feeling of foolishness clouding her judgement.

"Well, you've got a week to mull it over," said her friend, "See how you feel then. Now, let me tell you about the Samhain festival we've got coming up next month…"

Chapter ThirtyFour. Charlotte.

Charlotte adjusted the circular ring light, tightening the wingnut to keep it in the perfect position. The light had been an investment as she wanted to present herself as professionally as possible.

She looked at the wall clock. Five minutes to nine. Charlotte looked in a small compact mirror as she applied lipstick in a deep purple shade. She then brushed through her dyed black hair and picked off a couple of stray hairs from her black jumper.

She quickly reread a couple of messages that she'd been sent earlier and made sure her candles were within reach.

Positioning her tablet in front of her on the dark wooden dining table, she took a deep breath and pressed the 'Go live' button. Smiling broadly at the camera, Charlotte silently whispered, 'Showtime.'

"Good evening folks. Love and light to all," she began, "I'll just wait for a few more of you to hop on before I begin."

Glancing at the viewing figure in the corner she saw it said five. Scanning the names she continued,

"Hello Margaret, good to see you again. Hello Brian, welcome, love and light to you. Tracy, hope you had a good holiday, we missed you. If any of you could press the 'share' button I would be eternally grateful. Hello Christine, hello Annabelle. Love and light to you all."

Charlotte smiled broadly as a flurry of red love hearts floated upwards on her screen.

" The energies are high tonight, I can feel them. Remember, if you would like a personal reading or spiritual guidance you can become a supporter by following the link below. That's five pounds per month for exclusive access to special lives and the chance of personal readings or guidance."

Charlotte struck a match and lit a purple candle.

" I'm lighting a purple candle for wisdom tonight as I'm seeking answers for a couple of questions I've been sent.

Hello Stella, hello Diane, hello Jaspar, love and light to you all on this special night."

The candle flame danced and flickered adding to the magical atmosphere that Charlotte was creating.

" Hello to you Adriana, beautiful name. Hello Sean, good to see you back, hope the leg is healing well. Hello Marie, love and light to each and every one of you. I feel blessed by you taking the time to message."

She looked at the viewing figures. They were in the high twenties now.

" Ok, welcome all. I am so grateful for each and everyone of you here tonight. Something led you here and I believe it's because the universe has answers for those who seek its wisdom." Charlotte changed her expression to one of earnest concentration as she spoke again,

"I'm going to start by thanking the Goddess and the Ancients." She lit a white candle, dipped her fingers in a white bowl of water on which floated white rose petals. She dripped water on both sides of the candle saying, "Goddess of the New Moon, I thank you for your constant presence. Be our protection and our guide. By fire and waters blessed essence."

Lowering her head, Charlotte stayed silent for a moment before she looked up and smiled.

"Ok. I can see people still joining us, welcome.

I've received an email from Alice in Colne. Alice wants to know if she will find love with a certain man in her workplace. I won't say his name, but the powers know exactly who he is. Alice, love, I'm going to do my special attraction spell. It's powerful magic and I've never had it fail yet."

Charlotte made a motion with her hand to emphasize the point.

"I've written your name and the man in question on pieces of paper Alice, and now I'm going to bind them together."

Charlotte rolled up the slips of paper into a small scroll and tied them together with red wool. She then lit a long, red, dinner candle and placed it in a brass holder on the table.

"Let these two souls be bound together as their names are bound with thread. I light a red candle, to evoke passion and love for each other in these two souls. Let the universe and all the powers of the wind, water, fire and earth cause it to pass."

Taking the scroll in her hands, Charlotte then theatrically drew it through the candle flame quick enough for it not to catch alight. She then placed the scrolls in a jam jar and screwed on the lid.

"I'll keep this under a rose quartz crystal in my scriing room. Love and light to you Alice," Charlotte said to the screen, smiling broadly, "Let me know when the wedding is."

Another flurry of hearts danced up the screen.

"Don't forget folks. For five pounds a month subscription, you can be a supporter of my channel and have exclusive access to seances, and be entered into monthly draws for personal tarot readings and incantations. Just follow the link below," Charlotte made a downward motion with her index finger.

" Can anyone else feel the energy tonight?" she asked," It feels very powerful. I know it's a new moon. "

A further flurry of thumbs up emojis and hearts.

" Ok, I've had another email from Diane in Colchester. Love and light to you Diane. Diane tells me she has a problem with her neighbours cat. "

An hour and a half later and Charlotte had finished her live and blown out the candles.

She switched off the ring light and tidied away before walking into the living room.

" Alright love?" asked her husband Joe, looking up from the tv. Charlotte sat down with a sigh,

" Yes, was a good night. Twelve new subscribers and a couple of good donations. Should be able to book that trip to Disneyland soon. My viewing figures are going through the roof! Kids asleep?"

Joe smiled appreciatively, "Good stuff! Yeah, out like lights. Shall I make us a brew?"

"Oooo, yes please," Charlotte replied, "I'm gasping. Couple of choccie biscuits would go down a treat too."

Joe grinned, "Coming right up for my clever wifey."

Chapter ThirtyFive.
Payback.

Charlotte was busy on the desktop computer in the living room, answering emails from followers of her page. Her hair was tied up, off her face that was devoid of makeup. On the white desk in front of her sat a china mug of coffee and a saucer with two chocolate digestive biscuits.

As Charlotte tapped away at the keyboard, she heard a soft knock at the door. Leaving her computer mid email, she went to see who it was who had interrupted her work.

She walked down the hallway barefoot and could see a silhouette of someone through the frosted glass panel of the pvc front door. On opening the door, she smiled in recognition, "Hello, what brings you here?" she asked curiously.

"Can I come in. I need your help again?" he asked with a sorrowful look on his face.

Charlotte looked worried, "Of course, come in," she said opening the door wider and gesturing for him to come into the house.

He wiped his feet carefully on the mat and walked down the hall to the living room.

"Sit down," said Charlotte, "What's this all about?"

He sighed loudly, not knowing quite how to begin. "Could I have a glass of water?" he asked licking his dry lips.

Frowning, Charlotte nodded and went to the kitchen sink to fill a glass.

Suddenly, she dropped the glass, shattering it in the stainless steel sink as he pulled a length of cable tight around her neck from behind. She tried to prise the cable free frantically but couldn't get her fingers underneath. Then she tried to claw behind her at his face and hands. He easily dodged her hands with his head but she did manage to dig her sharp nails into the skin of his hands. The cable tightened. The pressure felt like her head would explode. White dots of light danced before her eyes before, after what seemed such a long time, everything finally went black.

The man dragged Charlotte's lifeless body back into the living room, her bare feet leaving two parallel lines in the thick pile if the almost new carpet, and sat it in one of the silver grey armchairs. He checked for a pulse. None.

He went back into the kitchen for a knife. Selecting a serrated carving knife, he took it from the kitchen drawer. Seeing the coloured candles on the counter top, he chose a white one together with the brass candlestick and returned to the living room.

Charlotte lay slumped on the chair, her head lolling to one side and her eyes staring at nothing. He knew that he had plenty of time before anyone would be home. The visitor had researched the life of Charlotte Redferne well. He took out his burgundy, pocket bible and began to read,

"Micah, Chapter five, verse ten.

'In that day', declares the Lord, 'I will destroy your horses from among you and demolish your chariots. I will destroy the cities of your land and tear down all your strongholds. I will destroy your witchcraft and you will no longer cast spells.' "

The visitor made the sign of the cross and then kissed the bible before reverently placing it on the mantlepiece.

He then lit the white candle, fixed it into its brass candlestick and placed it next to the bible.

Pulling off Charlotte's jeans he prayed in his native tongue as he worked. Methodically, he removed each item of her clothing and folded them neatly into a pile on the silver grey carpet. He then removed his own clothing and folded each item likewise.

Now fully naked, he gently picked up the knife and knelt before Charlotte's body. He reached over and pulled her tongue out from between her dead lips. Holding it with one hand, he sawed through the fibrous tissue with the knife until he held it, dripping and detached. Blood pooled in Charlotte's mouth until it spilled over her lower lip in narrow, dark red rivers.

He then began to remove Charlotte's eyes from their sockets with a twisting slicing motion of the knife.

Next, he got to work on her hands. With not a little effort, he gradually separated each hand from each wrist, adjusting his cutting angles to seperate the bones at the joints. The carpet became covered with coagulating blood as he worked until, when he finally stood, two clean patches remained where his knees had knelt.

He found a carrier bag in one of the kitchen cupboards and put the two hands, the slippery eyeballs and the flaccid tongue inside. He looked down at himself, blood spatter covering his stomach and legs, and realised he needed a shower. Climbing the stairs heavily, he looked into doors on the landing. First a pretty pink room with a white cot and a mobile with fluffy sheep dangling from a cross shaped frame. The next room was decorated with a space theme. Blue and yellow, planets, spaceships and stars. Lego and toy cars sat on the top of a bookcase full of encyclopedias and science books. Liam passed by these showing no trace of emotion. The third door was the family bathroom. He stepped into the shower and washed away the blood and pieces of gore that had stuck to his skin. Once clean, he dried himself on a soft, sky blue towel he found in the airing cupboard, before descending the stairs and getting dressed. Putting his bible in his jacket pocket, then picking up the carrier bag of flesh, he left the house, making sure he closed the front door behind him.

Chapter ThirtySix.
Speechless.

Blue light pulsed through the window onto the grim scene inside the lounge of the semi detached house.

"Close those curtains, for God's sake!" shouted DI Johnson angrily, "The whole bloody world and his wife will be rubber necking at the poor woman!"

PC Sarah Preston obediently drew the silver grey taffeta curtains.

"Where's the husband?" Johnson said less angrily.

"Upstairs, with the kids," replied Preston, "John Carpenter is up there with them."

"Good, PC Carpenter can act as FLO on this one. I think a male family liason could work better," said the DI, "Do we know where the other body parts are?"

DS Rasheed shook his head, "No sign of them so far. Looks like the killer may have taken them with him or her?"

DI Johnson frowned. Why? Why the eyes, the tongue and the hands?

He peered at the cable around Charlotte's throat. It was almost hidden as it was pulled so tightly into the flesh of her neck.

" Strangulation by ligature," he remarked to no one in particular, "Same MO as Greta Gray but more over kill here. As though he's escalating his killings."

"You think it's the same killer?" asked Rasheed.

"We've got to keep all lines of enquiry open, but same ligatures, both women of a similar age." replied Johnson.

SOCO Jones was taking photographs of the scene. His assistant was labelling any blood stains found in the room.

"It's looking highly likely that both women were killed by the same man, but there are key differences so I can't be certain. To have two strangulation killers in the same town would be very unusual." Jones explained, "The cutting of the wrists is definitely post mortem as there's zero evidence of arterial spray. My guess is that the tongue and eyes were post mortem also. We'll run more tests, back at the mortuary."

DS Rasheed looked around the room. He walked over to the computer desk in the corner. Looking at the full, now cold mug of coffee and uneaten biscuits, he called over the DI.

" Looks like she may have been on the computer shortly before the murder. We could power it up and check the times etc." he conjectured.

"We'll take it back to the station and get the tech guys on it," said Johnson, "Good work Abdul."

The next morning, after speaking with Charlotte's husband, DI Johnson had learned of Charlotte Facebook business page and obtained her passwords. He was now sat with Jakub Kowalski, looking intently at the screen of the desktop computer taken from the Redferne home.

Watching the recordings of Charlotte's lives, felt strangely intrusive to Ian. Seeing the woman on the screen, youthful and full of life, and knowing she was the same person as the mutilated body he'd seen at the house felt very uncomfortable.

"There are at least sixty similar video's saved in her files," Jakub explained to the DI in his heavy Polish accent.

Jakub Kowalski had worked with Ian for around seven years now. He was the 'go to' man for any tech issues. Jakub Kowalski worked magic with computers and was able to break the most complicated security systems and retrieve deleted images and messages with ease.

He'd lost count of the times he'd been called over with a, "Hey, Kowalski!" in a New York accent, but he took it all in good humour. In his mid-forties, Jakub had lived in the UK since the age of twenty five, when he left his native Poland as an economic migrant, seeking a better life for himself in comparison to the poverty his homeland offered. He'd worked hard and studied hard, and now was a longstanding and valuable member of constabulary staff.

Jakub had managed to find the Facebook messages sent to Charlotte on her business page. Most were requests for help or thanks, but a few were less friendly in tone. Trolling comments on lives and very personal verbal attacks in Charlotte's direct messages. Could one of these be Charlotte's attacker?

The DI called over PC Preston. Sarah Preston joined the two men looking at the computer screen.

"Sarah , I want you to work with Jakub on this one. We need ID's and if possible, addresses for these people who messaged Charlotte Redferne prior to her murder.

"Yes sir," she replied and wheeled over an office chair to begin work.

Sarah Preston was twenty six years old and dedicated to her work. A real asset to the force. DI Johnson could see a great deal of potential in the young PC and foresaw a rapid rise up the ranks in the not too distant future.

She was a striking woman with her dark, glossy hair and the most piercing, feline eyes.

Sarah Preston was extremely inquisitive and would seize any opportunity to try to understand the workings of the criminal mind and the puzzles of detective work. She relished this opportunity of working with the murder squad. She'd always been fascinated by what some might call the 'darker', side of life, but Sarah saw it as learning about the human condition across a wide spectrum of behaviours, influences and vulnerabilities.

Her curious nature had meant she had excelled at school as she absorbed knowledge with a passion. This gave her a level of wisdom more in keeping with someone years older. Her maturity and emotional intelligence helped enormously in the more difficult aspects of the job. Jakub briefed her on his findings to date as Sarah made comprehensive notes on a spiral bound notebook. The remainder of the afternoon they spent happily collating information together as they drank coffee.

Chapter ThirtySeven. Shock.

Eve was rinsing lettuce for a salad, shaking the copper collander under the running tap. She wore a flowing, purple maxi dress with elbow length sleeves, a long strand of multi coloured gemstones around her neck and she had tied a multi coloured silk scarf round her head as a headband. "There's been another one," Ian said as he entered the kitchen, removing his grey suit jacket.

"Another murder? Oh my God!" said Eve, turning away from the sink and bringing her hand to her mouth as she spoke, "Same killer?"

"It's a distinct possibility," said her husband, "This one was a young woman in her own home. She had two kids as well, thank God they weren't home. Her husband is in pieces. Make sure you always keep the doors locked Eve. You never know who's about."

Eve nodded and dried her hands on a checked tea towel.

Ian poured himself two fingers of his scotch, drank them straight down and then poured another.

" Do you have any suspects? " asked Eve playing nervously with the smooth beads of her necklace.

" We're following up some leads but no one obvious," Ian replied.

Eve rubbed her husbands back with the palm of her hand in a soothing gesture. He put an arm protectively around his wife's shoulders, "He's escalating Eve, getting more violent. We need to catch him soon."

Usually ready with the right words to say in any situation, Eve was silent. She put her arms around her husbands neck and held him close. She was worried, and she could tell Ian was too.

The front door opened and their son, Joel walked in.

" Hi parents. Am just going to shower and change and then I'm meeting Molly for a drink and something to eat at the Kettledrum," Joel informed them.

"Ok, make sure you get a cab back though Joel," said Eve.

"Will do mamma," he replied, climbing the stairs two at a time to the bathroom.

Eve broke away from her hug and returned to making the salad. Ian went to sit in the wicker chair the overlooked the garden. It was going dark already. The gloom of twilight gave the sky a heather purple tinge. The new moon was peeping behind grey clouds and the solar lights were glowing in the borders. He could see the swift swooping arcs of bats flying beneath the branches of the trees. It would soon be too cold for the midges and moths that provided meals on the wing for the tiny pipistrelles.

Looking out, over the garden, helped Ian unwind. He never tired of the ever-changing tableau outside the french doors. Year to year, season to season, even hour to hour, the view changed. The garden calmed his soul as it slowly, but constantly, renewed itself. He sipped the scotch, enjoying the peaty, smoky taste. He savoured each mouthful, keeping the amber gold liquid on his tongue, before it slipped down his throat, warming and soothing.

Joel reappeared in the kitchen smelling of soap and paco rabanne 1 million. His short, brown hair was waxed and styled and he was dressed in wine coloured tapered chinos that stopped just above his ankle and casual canvas shoes without socks. A lightweight, stone coloured sweater completed the look. He flashed a perfect white smile, before exchanging goodbyes with his parents and getting into his waiting cab.

Eve plated quiche and new potatoes onto two plates setting them down on opposite sides of the large, wooden table. She then brought the bowl of salad and a jug of water and placed them in the centre. The glasses and cutlery were there already, so Ian and Eve sat down to eat. They almost always sat at the table together for dinner. It was a time to talk about their day and was a routine that kept each of them in touch with the others feelings and moods and helped keep their relationship strong.

They ate and discussed light topics. It would do no good to let murder colour the whole of their conversation and they both knew that enough had been said on that subject for one day. There was enough of that at work for Ian, home was a place to relax.

After dinner, Ian made them both an Irish coffee and they listened to music as they drank them, curled up on the mustard, velvet sofas in the lounge. A real fire burned in the grate and the couple were happy in each others company.

By ten, Ian and Eve went upstairs and made gentle, unhurried love before they fell asleep, Eve's head resting on her husband's bare chest. They were dead to the world by the time Joel let himself into the darkened house, locked the beautiful, Edwardian front door and took himself to bed.

Eve sat on her yoga mat in the lotus position with her eyes closed. She wore loose, navy blue yoga pants and a purple, vest top. Her firey hair was piled messily on top of her head, curly tendrils escaping and spiralling over her ears. She had just finished her stretches and now she would perform her salutation to the sun.

Ian was upstairs in the shower. Lathering his salt and pepper hair as he tried to figure out a connection, if there was one, between the two killings. He went over the details in his head, looking for connections. They were a similar age, sex, ethnicity, but apart from that? Why did the killer target those two? Was it random? There didn't seem to be a sexual or robbery motive.

He rinsed off his hair and stepped out of the shower, rubbing his body with the large, grey bath sheet that had been warming on the towel rail.

After spraying anti perspirant, Ian walked naked through to the bedroom where he selected work clothes for the day and dressed. Downstairs, Eve put ground coffee into the machine and switched it on. As the coffee noisily bubbled through the filter, Eve put multi seeded bread into the copper coloured toaster. She then busied herself getting cups, saucers, butter and milk out in preparation. The toast popped up just as Ian came into the kitchen. His wife buttered the four slices and poured the coffee.

They sat together at the chunky, teak dining table and ate their breakfast. By the second piece of toast, a yawning Joel appeared with mussed up hair, "Morning parents," he said tiredly.

"There's coffee in the pot," said his mother, smiling.

Joel muttered a muffled thanks through another yawn and poured himself a cup.

"Dad? Any chance of borrowing some petrol money 'til Friday?" Joel asked Ian meekly.

"Sure," replied his father, opening his wallet and taking out a twenty pound note.

Joel rarely asked, he didn't like to, so both parents were happy to help out when he did. Ian handed his son the money with a smile, "You home for dinner tonight?"

"Think I'm meeting Molly straight after work so no," replied Joel, sitting down at the table with them. "I'm due at a customer's at nine-thirty to fit a gas fire, so I've time for breakfast today," he grinned.

"It's good that your kind of work can be flexible. Gives you more freedom," said Eve, "And people are always going to need plumbers."

"Always good to have a trade," added Ian, "Am proud of you son."

Joel nodded, drank a couple of gulps of coffee and then went to see what kinds of cereals were in the wall cupboard. Joel had a mild foetal alcohol syndrome which had made life more difficult for him. Ian and Eve had adopted him, and his elder sister, Yasmin, when he was a small child. They'd always supported and loved him and given him the confidence to set goals. He'd finished his apprenticeship last year and then worked hard to become Corgi registered. He was now self employed. Still building his reputation, he was far from rich, but more happy customers, meant more recommendations and the steady growth of his business.

Joel sat back at the table, with his bowl of cornflakes and a second cup of coffee.

"Any nearer catching that murderer, pops?" asked Joel between mouthfuls.

Ian sighed, "Not really," Ian admitted, "We're still following leads but no obvious suspect yet."

"You'll get him," Joel said encouragingly.

"Am sure he will," agreed Eve.

Ian hoped so. He needed to.

Ian stood, "Well I better go do some police work then and catch the bugger," he answered, smiling at his son warmly. Slipping his arms into his jacket, Ian kissed his wife goodbye, gave a farewell wave to Joel, and walked determinedly out of his home and into his car.

Chapter ThirtyEight. Press.

It was a cold, October evening. The jaundice yellow glow from the street lamps lit the road with pools of amber. The gritters were already out in force as freezing temperatures had been forecast overnight. Liam had just finished work at the warehouse and stopped at the newsagents for cigarettes on his way home. He was in a rush as he only had an hour or so before he started his pizza delivery shift. Fumbling in his pocket for change, he almost stumbled backwards. His eyes grew wide as he saw the familiar face of Charlotte Redferne with her husband and the two chidren, all smiling out of the front page of the newspaper like some macabre souvenir of happier times. He felt compelled to buy it.

After paying for the cigarettes and the newspaper, Liam ran out of the shop, in a hurry to get home. Quickly putting on his helmet and climbing onto his bike, he started her up and twisted the throttle. Rushing home to read the write up of the killing, he roared through the darkness and down the road, racing through amber lights in his hurry. Liam's heart was pumping in his chest almost as fast as it had at Charlotte's house. He laughed as he wove through the traffic, horns beeping at his recklessness. This was exciting! He was getting the recognition for the Lord's work! They would all see, they would all know, as they finally did at Ninevah, that they had to turn away from their sin, repent of their wickedness before it was too late. Breaking the speed limit, he almost ran over a black cat as he turned a corner, just missing the poor thing by an inch. Slowing down a little, realising there was no need to break his neck racing home, he began to ride more carefully.

Arriving at the front of his little flat, he leapt off the bike grabbing his keys, jumped over the grass verge and hurried inside.

He began to read through the story, and then he frowned.

"His ways are higher. His wisdom is greater than Liam's, we cannot question the Almighty. We can't see the end, only the beginning, He knows the beginning and the end of all things," said Liam to himself. He'd been talking to himself quite a lot recently.

He stood, re-reading through the piece. He was right, much of his work had been ignored. His work bore witness to his mission for Christ. It was important. Where were the details? Where were the facts? It was important that people knew the whole story or how would they repent of their folly?

Feeling the anger growing inside, he knew he needed to calm down. He forcibly slowed his breathing and dug his nails into his palms. Sitting down in his favourite chair, Liam needed to think. There was so much work still to do. So much work, and he would do it, and willingly, but first, there were pizzas to deliver.

A tired Liam put his helmet back on and set off to his second job of the day. Four hours of stuffed crust pepperoni and various other pizzas later, Liam rode wearily home, exhausted and ready for sleep.

Once in the flat, Liam sat in his chair and ate his free margherita, washed down with a glass of tap water.

After his meal, as he sat in the quiet, cold room, he could hear the scratching sound again. He heard it more often now, usually when he was in bed at night.

Scritch, scratch, scritch.

Scritch, scratch, scritch.

It was coming from his mother's room. He knew what it was. It was Cheryl, scratching at the door with her manicured nails.

Scritch, scratch, scritch.

Scritch, scratch, scritch.

The noise kept him awake. He tried to block up his ears with cotton wool but he could still hear it. It was incessant.

Scritch, scratch, scritch.

Scritch, scratch, scritch.

The cold air in his lungs each night had given him a hacking cough. Spluttering, he coughed up green phlegm and spat it onto the floor. He listened. Silence. The coughing had made her stop. He exhaled and relaxed.

Then,

Scritch, scratch, scritch.

Scritch, scratch, scritch.

"ARRGHHH," he screamed into the air, pulling at his hair, "SHUT UP! SHUT UP!"

Covering his ears with his hands, tears squeezing out from his eyes screwed shut, he began to rock backwards and forwards.

"Shut up, shut up, shut up."

Scritch, scratch, scritch.

Scritch, scratch, scritch.

Chapter ThirtyNine. Spells.

It was Saturday. Not just any Saturday, but a Saturday heralding a new moon. The perfect night for a bit of revenge magic.

She waited until almost midnight, the witching hour, that stupid prick Chris wouldn't know what hit him.

She'd gathered all the things she needed. A black candle, candlestick, matches, a knife and a smooth black pebble.

Calling on the four elements of wind and water, fire and earth, she carefully carved his name into the side of the candle then set it in a candlestick, struck a match and lit it.

She watched the flickering, yellow flame grow taller and begin to melt the wax. She stared transfixed by the flame as hot globules of wax began to spill over the edge of the candle and roll down its sides before solidifying once more as they lost their heat. As the candle burned slowly down, Sarah waited, impatiently, until the flame began to lower, melting through the carved letters.

At the perfect moment, she blew out the candle and poured the well of hot wax over the round black stone. Taking the knife, she carved a C into the soft wax as it began to solidify on the cool, sea-worn smooth surface of the pebble.

It was done. The spell was cast. Sarah smiled to herself and feeling suddenly exhausted, went to bed.

Sunday morning. It had rained overnight but the morning was dry and crisp.

Chris almost bounced out of bed and into the shower, leaving the blonde who he thought might be called Amy or maybe Emmie, asleep in his bed.

He brushed his teeth in the shower, then got dressed in his leathers. Scribbling a quick note,

'Thanks for last night hun, was great. Just pull the door to as you leave, ta x,' he left it on his pillow and went downstairs to his beloved T120.

Putting on his helmet he took a deep lung full of the brisk morning air, feeling good.

Straddling the bike, he walked it out of the lock up and started the engine. He loved the sweet low growl of her engine. Setting off out of the car park, he smiled to himself.

It really was a beautiful day. The pale sun over the hills, lending a golden tone to the landscape. The sky a clear Tiffany blue with just the odd wisp of cloud. He rode through the town and onto the Todmorden Road. Houses gave way to rolling fields and the deep cut through the valley where the road followed the stream. The sun shone, drying the damp roads as it made them blinding white with reflected glare. A wiser man would have slowed his pace but Chris was loving the thrill of the ride. The corners were tight and many and he tilted the bike until his knee almost grazed the tarmac at each turn, feeling like a competitor at the Isle of man TT. He swung the bike to the right and then to the left, leaning into each curve of the road. Past sheep grazing on a slope so steep it was cliff like, past farmhouses and drystone walls. He roared along the road, the Triumph taking it all in its very British stride.

After seven miles of breathtaking countryside, he arrived in Todmorden itself, and parked up by a little biker pub he often frequented. Taking off his helmet, he ordered a pint of lager and a burger. He took them outside, to the picnic style benches set on the stone paved forecourt. The burger was excellent. Handmade of good quality steak from local cows and seasoned perfectly. The day was getting better and better. Taking another bite, he saw a blonde girl in tight, black leathers looking in his direction. He smiled politely and she smiled back with a flutter of her long eyelashes. Her lips were painted a deep red and her ash blonde hair was poker straight and blew gently in the slight breeze.

He took another bite of his burger, chewing more slowly now as he studied the curve of her backside covered in the figure hugging leather.

She flicked her hair from her face with a hand sporting red talon like nails, and shot him a killer smile.

Finishing the burger, he wiped his mouth with the paper serviette and picking up his glass, walked over to the leather clad queen. He began an easy conversation about bikes and torque. She was very knowledgeable which he found incredibly sexy. He found he focused on her painted mouth as she spoke, imagining those soft, red lips sliding down the hard shaft of his erect cock.

He risked putting an arm around her waist and found she smiled at the move.

Sensing no resistance, he moved in for a kiss.

"What the fuck!" growled a low voice behind him. He turned just in time to see the broken beer bottle being pushed into his face by a bearded giant of a man in Hell's Angels leathers.

Chris clutched his hands to his face as his blood poured down from the jagged wounds on his forehead, temporarily blinding him. He felt another thrust of glass into flesh and an audible pop accompanied by white hot pain as his right eyeball was pierced.

Sinking to the floor, he heard screams as the woman held back her furious boyfriend. They then both climbed onto a Honda Goldwind and roared away down the country road.

Chris felt nauseous and vomited the gourmet burger onto the stone paving as he sat slumped against the pub wall. Blood running down and pooling on the stone floor as he lost conciousness and someone phoned for an ambulance.

Chapter Forty. Disfigured.

It had been a long day, in terms of workload as well as hours. The murders meant everyone was working extra hard trying to find answers. Any leave previously booked was cancelled for the forseeable and it was all hands to the pumps.

It was bad enough when it was just the one murder, but two killings in such a short amout of time was frightening for the general public and the team were under intense pressure to find answers. The Chief Inspector Ruth Emmerson was breathing heavily down the neck of DI Johnson. This meant he was in ultra serious mode, verging on bad tempered, as he struggled to find useful lines of enquiry. DS Rasheed was feeling the pressure too and this filtered down the ranks, also affecting the less senior members of staff. They all just had to keep their heads down and do their jobs well until they found that vital piece of evidence that would lead them to the killer. Sarah hoped they would find something positive to work with soon.

She drove her orange fiat to the supermarket to pick up something for tea, at least that's what she told herself. In reality she was going for a nice bottle of red to counteract the stresses of the day, but felt guilty going shopping solely for alcohol so she picked up a tub of ready made Arrabbiata sauce and a potted basil plant along with a bottle of shiraz that was on special offer.

Glad to finally arrive home from the supermarket, Sarah put some pasta on to boil and opened the tub of spicy Arrabbiata sauce which she popped in the microwave to heat through. She grated some parmesan into a small bowl and then drained the pasta. Mixing the pasta and sauce together, she then poured the mixture onto a plate and sprinkled some torn basil leaves and parmesan on top.

She ate her pasta as she scrolled through Facebook posts on her phone.

She had almost finished her meal when she googled the town newspaper's site to check out the crime stories locally.

Reading through the headlines, she suddenly stopped chewing and dropped her fork onto the white plate with a clatter. Permanently disfigured? Sarah read the words on her phone and felt sick. She swallowed the final mouthful of food but it felt too big, as though it would stick in her throat and went down slowly and painfully. She read it through again.

'Local man, Christopher Jameson, 29, was viciously attacked as he visited a pub in Todmorden for Sunday lunch. Keen bike enthusiast, Mr. Jameson, lost an eye and suffered significant damage to his forehead and cheek in the unprovoked attack which will leave the talented software developer permanently disfigured. A witness told our reporter, "There was blood everywhere, his eye was just hanging out. The fella that glassed him was a big biker with a beard and 'Hells Angels,' on the back of his jacket."

Police are looking for information. If you witnessed Sunday's attack or have any informa… '

Oh my God! I didn't expect him to be permanently disfigured. She felt pangs of remorse and blame. Normally, she wasn't the vengeful type, he had just made her so angry with his arrogant attitude, as though he were God's gift. It probably would have still happened without the spell, she rationalised, but couldn't quite shift the ill at ease feelings in the pit of her stomach.

Getting a bundle of white sage from a kitchen drawer, she lit it and placed it in the pretty, oil on water coloured, abalone shell so that the cleansing smoke would remove any negative energy from her home. Then she placed ground ginger, basil and cinnamon in a jar. Plucked some if the petals from the white chrysanthemums she had in a vase and added them to the jar. Lastly, she put in a few silver nails and topped up the jar with water. She shook the jar to mix so all the elements swirled around in the water and spoke an incantation asking for protection.

Feeling slightly better, she poured herself a glass of wine, and sat on her sofa with her legs tucked underneath her to sip it slowly. Was it the spell? It can't have been. She didn't want him hurt like that. It must have been a coincidence. She was being silly thinking burning a candle would cause such a terrible thing. She took a sip of her wine and decided she would give any dark magic a wide berth from now on.

She switched on the tv and tried to find something light and cheerful to watch. Settling on a comedy, she watched tv and drank her wine. The fragrant aroma of the burning sage drifted through the flat, causing Sarah to relax and she soon forgot all about Chris Jameson and his hanging eyeball.

Chapter FortyOne. Family.

Rose lay naked on the crisp white sheet, her eyes closed, her mouth slightly open and her chin tilted up. Her knuckles were white as she tightly gripped the bars of the wrought iron bedstead behind her head. She let out a low moan as she tilted her hips towards Yasmin's mouth. Yasmin's tongue lapped at the swollen pink pearl of her clitoris with lengthy, slow movements driving her girlfriend wild with desire. Yasmin gradually increased the pressure and speed, listening for her partner's moans as cues, until, when Rose arched her back and her moans became louder and more insistent, Yasmin's tongue flicked quickly and firmly away bringing Rose to a shuddering orgasm. Yasmin then pulled away, inserting two fingers into the hot, velvety soft wetness between Rose's legs and thrusting them in an out, her knuckles meeting the solid resistance of Rose's pelvic bone as she went deep with each stroke. Yasmin watched the expressions of pleasure on her girlfriend's face, enjoying the effect her fingers were creating. Yasmin curled her fingers slightly as she worked, intensifying the feelings of pleasure for Rose, who tilted her pelvis up to Yasmin's wet hand and squirmed in delirious ecstacy. Yasmin's fingers continued their rythmic thrusting deeper still, the low, liquid noises of Rose's arousal emanating from inside her hot sex, stimulating Yasmin's own clitoral responses by sheer empathetic eroticism.

"Yes, yes!" Rose cried out as a rush of fluid covered Yasmin's hand and the electric spasms of orgasm coursed through Rose's body. Rose sat up and hurriedly pushed Yasmin onto her back, switching positions and lowering her head whilst looking deep into Yasmin's beautiful eyes, began greedily eating her girlfriend's eager sex, reddened and wet with arousal. Yasmin's eyes widened and she grinned before biting her lower lip and letting out a gasp as she felt Rose's hot tongue find its mark.

Later, they were getting ready to go to Yasmin's parents.
Rose wore a black velvet tunic with lacing criss crossing over the v-neck. She matched this with black jeans and black pleather, ankle boots with a block heel. Her dyed, pastel pink hair was piled loosely

on her head in a messy bun and around her neck she wore a black velvet choker, from which hung a silver pentagram.

Yasmin wore a hand-printed cotton, maxi skirt in earthy tones, with a mustard cardigan unbuttoned over a rust coloured vest top and thick tan belt. Brown faux suede knee boots completed the outfit. Sterling silver and amber earrings dangled from her ears and her brown curly hair hung loose around her shoulders.

"Come on babe," called Yasmin carrying the birthday presents, "We're going to be late."

"And whose fault is that?" grinned Rose with a wink of her eye, as she locked the door to their little house.

Yasmin grinned back as she opened the passenger door of their vauxhall corsa, "Not my fault I can't keep my hands of you."

Laughing, Rose climbed into the driving seat, fastened her seat belt and began the countryside drive from Hebden Bridge to Burnley. They passed lush, green fields full of sheep and hillsides covered with purple heather. The landscape was beautifully wild and rugged. Before long, they'd crossed the border into Lancashire and were soon entering the outskirts of Burnley itself.

Turning into her inlaws drive, Rose parked the little, purple car and the two women got out. They walked up to the Edwardian front door, surrounded by original stained glass panels. Yasmin pressed the bell and the ringing sounded from inside. Through the glass they saw Eve appear wearing an emerald green silk shirt and black velvet leggings, closely followed by Ian in blue jeans and a loose white, cotton shirt.

"Come in, come in," said Eve gesturing with one hand and holding open the heavy front door with the other. Yasmin and Rose entered and were immediately given hugs by first Eve and then Ian.

Yasmin greeted Ian with, "Happy Birthday dad!" as she handed him two parcels wrapped in purple foiled paper.

Ian thanked both women and took the parcels to the kitchen table where he began to unwrap them.

"What would you like to drink?" Eve asked Rose and then Yasmin.

"Do you have juice? I'm designated driver today," Rose replied and Yasmin responded with, "White wine please."

Eve poured the women their drinks.

Ian had opened his gifts and was admiring the decanter and scotch. After thanking the two women they took their drinks into the lounge. Joel was already seated with his girlfriend, Molly on one of the mustard velvet sofas He stood up as they entered and hugged his sister and Rose and introduced them to Molly, who blushed slightly as they both welcomed her with yet another hug. Molly was a pretty girl of eighteen with strawberry blonde hair and freckles. She wore a burgundy a-line skirt with a roll neck jumper in a similar shade. Joel held her hand reassuringly, as he knew Molly would be a little nervous meeting more family members. This was Joel's first serious girlfriend and he felt very protective of her.

He wore jeans and a checked shirt with short sleeves rolled up above his growing biceps. He had started growing a beard which Molly thought suited him.

They chattered away as they drank their drinks, catching up on family news and finding out all they could about Molly, who soon overcame her shyness. They were a happy, friendly family and enjoyed the few times a year when they all gathered together.

"Ready to eat?" asked Eve and shepherded her family into the large kitchen diner. Ian refreshed their drinks as Eve placed steaming serving dishes of lentil chilli and rice on the heavy, reclaimed teak table. Another bowl of garden salad, a platter of garlic bread and a bowl of soured cream were placed wherever there was room and Eve invited the family to help themselves.

The chilli was delicious and Rose made a mental note to ask Eve for the recipe before they left.

Rose suddenly felt Ian's gaze fixed on her throat. She looked over at him, with a puzzled expression.

"A pentagram, not a star. A pentagram!" exclaimed Ian suddenly and excused himself to make a phone call. The remaining family looked at each other with quizical expressions and shoulder shrugs and continued eating.

Ian called the station and asked for DS Rasheed, "Abdul? It's Ian. The tattoo on Greta Grays hip. It wasn't a star, it was a pentagram. There's a link. Witchcraft. "

Chapter FortyTwo.Anger.

First, he was incredibly shocked and frightened. Now Chris was feeling angry. It bubbled through his veins, seething under his skin, like lava, waiting for the slightest crack to burst out of. It wasn't just the physical pain. It was the fact his vision and his looks had been destroyed. Would he be able to return to work? Would the scars make him repulsive to women?

On his arrival at the accident and emergency department at Blackburn hospital, he had undergone an unbelievably painful examination where they had forced open his eye to look inside. It felt as though they were probing his eye socket with red hot needles. After that, he had been taken almost straight away to theatre. It hurt so bad. The pain in his eye was excruciating, and the general anaesthetic came as welcome relief.

They couldn't save the eye so had decided to remove it and then they completed the delicate job of repairing the wounds in his skin, being extremely careful not to further damage any nerve endings that controlled the facial muscles.

It had taken hours of microsurgery to carefully remove splinters of glass and expertly stitch together the raw edges as best they could. His mother had arrived at the hospital as soon as she heard the news and was frantic with worry for her perfect son. Only now, he wasn't perfect, far from it. A few moments of violence had robbed him of so much.

As he came round from the anaesthesia, she cried and fussed around him until it almost drove him mad. In the end, the nurses had to tell her that he needed to rest for a few hours, just so he could get some relief from the constant questions interspersed with wailing and sobbing.

He had bandages covering most of his face for the first few days so she couldn't see the damage and he was glad of that for when they did unwrap them in front of her for the first time, he saw her actually recoil in horror at his appearance. She regained her composure quickly enough but it was too late, he'd seen her initial reaction and it scared him. He'd relied on his looks for most of his life. They helped him in job interviews, made attracting women effortless and meant friends were easy to find. He wasn't sure how to function in a world where he wasn't admired.

The fear had turned into resentment and the resentment had turned into pure rage.

He focused that anger on women. He had never had a lot of respect for women, but now, he despised them. It was that stupid blonde bint who had caused all this by giving him the come on despite already having a man. He seriously hoped they'd catch the fuckers who did this to him. He wanted them to pay.

They sent a psychologist to see him in hospital, a woman. She tried to ask how he felt about his injuries. He just looked at her through his one remaining eye like she'd just asked the stupidest question imaginable. His lip curled into a sneer and he refused to speak with her again.

Worse than that though, were the looks of pity. The nurses faces when they saw beneath the bandages enraged him. He had never been pitied in his life, envied yes, but never pitied.

Eventually, they let him go home. He was glad. Chris wanted to be left on his own, to stew in his own juice the more uncharitable might say. His mother drove him home and walked with him up to the large glass doors of the old church. He pressed in the door code numbers and heard the click of the door release. Sarah was coming down the stairs and stopped when she saw him. He went inside with his mother and gave her the dirtiest look he could muster with his single eye. She lowered her head and carried on out of the door without a word passing between them.

His mother was oblivious to the exchange, intent instead on getting her invalid son inside his flat and comfortable.

Turning his door key in the lock, he let them both in and his mother went straight for the kettle. She'd brought milk, bread and margarine with her.

Initially, she'd wanted Chris to stay with her, but he was adamant that he was going back to his own bed in his own flat. After making him a mug of tea, she went to put clean sheets on her son's bed. He let her get on with it, it was preferable than having to listen to her constant wittering.

After the sheets, it was the washing. She filled the machine and set it running. The noise of which he found extremely irritating. His nerves were jangling.

In the end, he ended up screaming at her,

"Mother! Can you please, for Christ's sake, let me have some fucking peace!

That did the trick. She snivelled a little, but picked up her bag and her coat, and finally left him alone.

After she'd gone, back to her neat and tidy semi detached, where his father had learned to just 'switch off,' from her incessant fussing, he threw the margarine in the bin and ordered an online shop to be delivered the next day that included his preferred brand of margarine and a decent bottle of vodka.

Chapter FortyThree.
Playdough.

It was a miserable, rainy day. Too wet to go anywhere exciting so the Brown household; Janet, Harry and little Amy were spending the day at home before the children went to Grandma Shauna's for their sleepover that night.

The children had already watched Frozen whilst Janet caught up with the housework and now, Harry and Amy were playing with playdough on the old dining table with their mum. Amy was just squishing it between her fingers and occasionally trying to eat it, but Harry was trying to roll a snake.

"Like this, Harry," Janet said, demonstrating how to roll her blue playdough.

Harry tried to copy his mum with his green playdough with less success, but he was slowly getting the hang of it. It wasn't far off Harry's fourth birthday and Janet was wondering what she should get him as a present. She was using this time spent playing with the children to try and fish for clues.

Poking eyes in her snake with a pencil, Janet casually mentioned the upcoming birthday.

"So Harry," she began, "If there was a magic fairy who said you could have one present for your birthday, what would you choose?"

Harry took the pencil next and began putting dozens of eyes onto his snake.

"Hmmm," said Harry, "I'm not sure."

"It could be anything, have a good think," Janet encouraged, "What would it be? I think I might choose some sparkly earrings or some new shoes. What would you choose, Harry?"

Harry was still poking eyes with an intense expression and his tongue poking out from between his rosy lips.

"Err, hummm," he stopped poking holes, looked up at the ceiling and put his right index finger on his chin, "hmmm, the moon?"

Janet laughed, "I can't get you the moon!"

"But you said a magic fairy, they could get the moon," he explained with a deadpan expression.

"True, I can't argue with that," conceded his mum, "What else?"

Harry struck his thinking pose again.

"Choc choc!" shouted Amy helpfully.

Laughing again, Janet agreed chocolate would be good, but waited for Harry to think of something.

"I know one thing I'd like," said Harry.

"Ok," said Janet, "And what's that?"

"I think," said Harry slowly.

Janet waited patiently.

"I think I want Darren to be my dad," he said to Janet, looking at her face expectantly.

"Yes! Darren," added Amy.

"Oh yes, you too," her brother said reassuringly.

Janet simply smiled. She could think of worse things to wish for.

They continued playing. Harry trying to make a moon and Janet showing him how to roll a ball.

Amy pressed her pencil into circles of playdough shouting, "Biscuit!"

As Janet moulded the dough, she pondered Harry's words and the more she thought about it, the better the idea seemed to be.

"Ok, let's get you two fed and then we can pack your overnight bags ready for grandmas," said Janet, "Put the playdough back in the tubs, and I'll put a pizza in the oven."

"Yay!" shouted both the children in unison at the mention of grandma's house. They loved their grandma and she always seened to have chocolate.

Harry did most of the tidying with Amy doing her best to help and then Janet picked up all the tiny, fiddly bits that ended up on the floor.

After pizza, chips and salad, the children excitedly packed their overnight bags with pyjamas, their favourite toy, their toothbrush and a change of clothes.

Braving the weather, the trip set off to catch the bus to grandma's house.

Harry looked out if the bus windows, quietly watching the world go by, Amy however, squirmed and wriggled on her mum's knee for the entire journey. After a short arguement over who was going ti ring the bell, it was a relief when they finally reached their stop.

Upon leaving the shelter of the bus, they ran through the driving rain, holding their hoods to try and keep from getting soaked through, then almost tumbled into the warm and dry of Grandma Shauna's bungalow, where she was ready to greet them with a beaming smile.

The return journey, on her own, was a much more pleasant experience. She could just sit and enjoy the ride.

A thoroughly soggy Janet arrived home around six thirty, and went straight upstairs to run herself a hot bath.

The children were safely dropped off at their great grandma's house, and Janet was going to take a bath before going round to Darren's house later that evening.

She loved a long soak. It was such a good time to relax and rebalance herself. Using the time productively, she was looking at online shopping sites on her phone. Harry wanted the moon for his upcoming birthday so she was wondering how best to arrange that. She found a cool, moon wall light with a remote control so that you could make the wall moon look in the same phase as the real moon. It took batteries so no wiring and hung on the wall the same way a picture would. That would be perfect!

Scrolling further, she found a colour-in-yourself, carboard rocket ship that was big enough to play inside. It was marked down to half price, eight and a half quid, so she put that in her online basket too. She ordered both items then put down her phone on the closed lid of the toilet, closed her eyes and lay back, enjoying the relaxing experience of perfect peace in her lovely, warm bath.

After twenty minutes or so, Janet reluctantly stirred herself. She shaved all offending growth from her body and then climbed out of the bath to begin getting ready to go to Darren's house.

Chapter FortyFour. Pizza.

Warm yellow light shone through the narrow gap in the curtains at the bay window of the terraced house. Janet climbed the three steps that led up to the black, painted door, and knocked, the sound muffled slightly by the burgundy woollen gloves she wore. The wind was whipping up a storm tonight, whistling through the trees in the parkland opposite and blowing litter across the pavements. The street was deserted. All sensible people were safe indoors, out of the biting wind, in the warmth of centrally heated living rooms drinking hot drinks and watching tv.

Harry and Amy were spending the night at her grandmother's house, giving Janet the opportunity to spend a full night at Darren's house. They had been so excited when she had dropped them off. They loved spending time with their great grandma Shauna, and the feeling was entirely mutual.

Janet stamped her feet against the cold and knocked again, "Hurry up Darren, it's freezing out here," she muttered to herself, pulling her woollen scarf higher up her face as the biting wind stung her cheeks.

The door finally opened and a smiling Darren, beckoned her inside. His feet were bare, and he wore black jeans and a black, 'Thrasher' T-shirt with the band's pentagram logo across the chest. He gave her a quick kiss on her cold cheek, then led her through to the living room, "Sorry I took a while, I was just taking a bin bag out."

A large, black leather corner sofa dominated the room and an enormous black tv hung from the opposite wall. The tv wall was painted matt black. Vintage posters in acrylic frames decorated the remaining walls which were painted a vibrant red. Brushed steel, wall picture lights illuminated each poster. The effect was decidedly masculine, a real man cave.

Janet took off her leather jacket and her gloves. She handed Darren a four pack of dark fruits cider then took a closer look at the posters; Judas Priest, Black Sabbath, Metallica, Iron Maiden. The illustrations on them were the stuff of nightmares. They depicted horned devils, grinning skulls, black mass crosses and other macabre imaginings.

"Have a seat," said Darren, "Tea or cider?"

"Guess," replied Janet grinning as she sat on the enormous sofa. She wore blue jeans and a wine coloured velvet shirt. A silver choker with tiny silver stars that dangled, catching the light, encircled her neck.

Darren poured Janet a chilled glass of the cider and sat down to drink his straight from the can.

His face suddenly serious, Darren whispered theatrically, "Erm, I have a confession."

Janet raised a quizzical eyebrow, "Oh?"

"I said I was going to cook," Darren continued, "but I haven't." He hung his head in mock humility.

"But I do have a pizza menu!" he exclaimed and gave an exaggerated grin.

Janet laughed, "Good thing I like pizza!"

She took the menu from his outstretched hand and scanned the list of topppings. They chose their pizzas, and Darren phoned through the order.

As they waited for their food, they found a movie on Netflix. A horror. Just the thing.

Curling up together on the sofa, they settled down to watch. The suspense was building, it was dark, the street was silent and the heroine looked terrified as she peeped around the corner.

Suddenly, "Brrring!" The doorbell rang and Janet screamed and nearly jumped out of her skin. Darren laughed as he stood up, "That'll be the pizza," he said, pausing the movie, still laughing as he went to answer the door.

"Alright mate!" Janet heard Darren say in a surprised tone, "Do you never sleep?" he joked, "Come through a minute," Darren said, motioning for the visitor to follow. Janet looked to the door wondering who he was talking to.

Darren returned to the living room, "Look who the pizza guy is!" Liam entered the room carrying the two pizza boxes, looking slightly uncomfortable.

"Liam!" squealed Janet, "Small world!"

"Yes, a small world it is," echoed Liam, looking around the red and black room.

"Do you want a drink, mate?" Darren asked Liam.

Liam shook his head, "No, no. I am working. I can't, but thank you."

"Ok, another time then. Thanks for these mate, I'll see you Monday," said Darren cheerily and walked Liam back to the front door.

"Bye Darren," Liam replied before putting his helmet back on and getting back on his motorbike.

Darren shut the door and returned to Janet, who had already opened her pizza box and was busy eating her first slice.

"You don't need a plate then," grinned Darren, settling back down on the sofa and opening his own pizza box. The pizza was good. Messy with lots of stringy hot cheese. They were soon full and Darren brought through damp paper towels to wipe the grease off their fingers.

They watched the remainder of the movie, Janet leaning against Darren's chest and his arm around her shoulder. Being together felt comfortable, it just felt 'right' thought Janet to herself. She felt his warmth and breathed in his scent, feeling relaxed and content. She softly kissed Darren's chest as they watched the movie, thankful to have him in her life.

After the movie, they made love. Unhurried and slow, enjoying each others bodies, safe in the knowledge that no child's voice would call from the upstairs landing, no worries about making too much noise. Just being together, alone in their own special world of sensuality and tenderness.

After each was sated, they went upstairs to bed, and fell into a deep, contented sleep, wrapped in each others arms and feeling the peace that comes from being in love.

Chapter FortyFive. Party.

They'd spent hours the night before wrapping pass the parcels, drawing out a 'pin the helmet on the spaceman' game on an old roll of wallpaper, filling party bags with sweets and bubbles and decorating the dining room with a space theme.

There were silver, blue and yellow balloons hung in groups of three around the room, dozens of silver stars were blue tacked to the walls, a crescent moon made from cardboard and tinfoil hung dangling from the central light fitting and flashing fairy lights were fastened around the window and door frames.

Harry was playing spacemen inside his cardboard rocket ship with Amy, which was set up in one corner of the room and Janet was busy making sandwiches in the kitchen. Darren put a black plastic tablecloth with silver stars all over it on the dining table and set out covered plates of jam tarts and fairy cakes with sugar stars.

Amy was dressed in a cute sky blue party dress with a ribbon sash and Harry had on a dress up spacesuit courtesy of Darren.

They had about twenty minutes before Harry's guests would arrive and Janet was feeling a little panicked. She gave Darren the job of slicing up a watermelon and putting the candles on Harry's space cake, as she finished up making the seemingly endless rounds of sandwiches and then covering them with clingfilm.

The doorbell rang, the first guests had arrived. Darren was in charge of the music with strict instructions that only bubblegum pop was allowed, NO heavy metal. Janet welcomed the first party guests, Daniel and Olivia. His dad Joe had come a few minutes early as he wanted to thank Janet for inviting them both so soon after their mum, Charlotte's murder. He hoped it would be good for them to have a bit of fun, as they hadn't had much lately. He was worried though, just how they would react, so he left his mobile number with Janet in case of any problems.

They stood, hiding behind their dad, looking wary and hesitant but Harry was straight over, inviting them into his rocket ship and they were soon laughing together as they caught hold of Harry and Amy's excitement. Joe was so relieved to see them smile and left feeling reassured. More guests arrived, dressed in their party finery and bearing gifts for the excited birthday boy. Once their respective mums and dads had gone, Janet began the first game of musical statues.

Darren was a surprisingly excellent DJ and Janet chuckled to herself when she caught him singing along to a Katy Perry song. Whenever Janet glanced over he was laughing and joking with all the children. He's a natural, thought Janet, and her heart melted a little more for her never boring and multi talented boyfriend. Another game, this time 'pin the helmet on the spaceman' which involved a blindfold that definitely got raised by a couple of little, cheeky cheaters when it was their turn. Soon, it was time for Janet to begin peeling the clingfilm off plates of food.

Smiling, she called the children to line up and handed out the party plates. They chose their sandwiches and goodies from the party table before sitting crosslegged on the floor to eat. Darren dished out paper cups of orange cordial and helped fill a binliner with used plates, cups and serviettes as each child finished.

Janet went into the kitchen to light the four stripey candles, before grandly carrying in the cake, nodding to Darren to switch off the lights as she went. Darren began the chorus of Happy Birthday and as Janet knelt down with the cake, a very happy Harry blew out the candles leaving the room dark until Darren quickly flicked the lightswitch.

Janet went back to the kitchen to wrap up slices of birthday cake in serviettes to add to the party bags, leaving Darren in charge of pass the parcel. One more game of wink murder to calm the mood.

The time seemed to fly by and Janet was caught by surprise as the first parent rang the doorbell.

Joe was so pleased when he saw his two children with beaming smiles chattering away about the party and he thanked Janet and Darren profusely for bringing a bit of light relief into their young lives. Soon, all the other parents came to collect their red faced, over excited offspring who left the party happy and carrying their party bags.

Janet shut the door behind the final child and his parents and gave an exaggerated sigh.

"Well, I think that went quite well!" she said and gave Darren a quick kiss on the lips, "Now let's get these two ready for bed and then it's grown up time," she said with a wink.

Darren caught her drift and grinned. He clapped his hands twice, "Right you two, go brush your teeth, and if you're back before I've vacuumed the floor, I'll read you a birthday story!"

Janet laughed as Harry ran up the stairs with Amy crawling up right behind him.

Chapter FortySix. Hate.

She was sat at the kitchen counter eating cornflakes with fresh raspberries and cold milk with an accompanying mug of tea. As she took a sip of the piping hot tea, Sarah mind wandered to Chris, downstairs. He absolutely detested her. She could tell that from the look he'd given her in the entrance hall on his return from his stay in hospital. His look had sent shivers down her spine as it was filled with such venom and poison.

His face was a mess, there was no getting away from that fact. An eye patch thankfully covered the empty left socket. The scars were still red and angry, but she could tell, that even when eventually faded to pink or silver, they would still dominate his face. His perfect face was destroyed forever. She felt guilt and pity in equal measure. How would she feel if it had happened to her, Sarah thought. Would she be angry and resentful like Chris? Did his terrible experience excuse his abysmal behaviour? She had to truthfully admit that she didn't know, but hoped that she would be less eaten up with hatred. Remembering the way he'd treated her at the end of their one and only date, however, tempered the feelings of pity somewhat.

Karma is a bitch, she thought to herself, excusing the revenge spell she herself had cast. Maybe time would mean acceptance for Chris and he would lose some of the bile.

Finishing her breakfast, she put the pots into the dishwasher and headed for the bathroom . A quick, hot, shower later and Sarah dressed in her uniform for work. She brushed her glossy hair back off her face and into a neat bun fastened with hair elastic and a couple of hairgrips.

She carefully applied her 'work' makeup of natural looking foundation and blush, no eyeshadow, a sweep of liquid eyeliner, mascara and nude lip. One final check of her reflection in the hall mirror and she was off out of the door and skipping down the stairs to her car.

Chris saw her leave from the window of his flat. "Bitch," he muttered to himself as he watched her get into her little car and drive away. Chris wouldn't be going to work that day. He was still on sick leave.

In the Johnson household, Ian had just stepped out of the shower and was rubbing his body dry with a large, grey bathsheet.

Wiping the condensation from the bathroom mirror, he studied his reflection critcally. He still had all his hair, but the salt was rapidly taking over from the pepper. He found odd eyebrow hairs that grew strangely long these days and now resorted to trimming them with scissors.

The laughter lines that used to disappear with his smile, now remained as permanent fine lines radiating out from the outer corners of his grey eyes. He was definitely feeling every one of his fifty years today.

After dressing in a navy suit and white shirt, Ian went downstairs for breakfast. A smiling Eve came over to him and kissed his lips which, in turn, made him smile.

He loved Eve, even after all these years, he still found her the most attractive woman he knew. He loved her caring nature and her creativity and imagination. He was so very grateful for her love and loyalty even when he was feeling the pressure of work, as he was now.

It seemed as though she could sense when work was getting a little too intense, Eve was very intuitive like that, and she made small changes to help him, such as preparing him a lush breakfast of smoked salmon and scrambled eggs as she had this morning. Sprinkled liberally with black pepper and with a wedge of lemon on the side, it was just what the doctor ordered. Eve brought the cafetiere of coffee to the table and then sat down opposite him to eat.

Squeezing lemon juice onto his salmon, Ian thanked his wife for the special breakfast.

"You're welcome," said Eve brightly, putting a fork full of salmon into her mouth.

They spent a good twenty minutes eating and talking together, and this kept their bond strong. They were each others best friend and biggest supporter and that made their marriage work. Joel appeared in the kitchen just as Ian was getting ready to leave, putting on his jacket and taking a final gulp of coffee.

"Morning son," he called on his way out of the door.

"Bye dad," Joel called after him before noticing the remnants of his parent's breakfast, "Ooo, smoked salmon, any left for your favourite son?"

Eve laughed, "Of course! Scrambled eggs with it?"

"Yes please, mum," Joel replied as he poured himself a glass of orange juice from the fridge.

Chapter FortySeven.
Profiling.

There had been two murders. One an attack on the street, the other, a home invasion and this missing person case. Were they linked?

DI Johnson and DS Rasheed were struggling to find a connection, excluding the fact that all were women living in the same locality. They were sat in Ian's office, going back through all the evidence. Two deaths by strangulation. One missing woman. Was there a connection or mere coincidence. It was time for some victim profiling. Also in the office, was criminal psychologist and lecturer, Angela Hewson, who the detectives had called in to help shed some light.

Professor Angela Hewson was an unassuming woman in her sixties. Years spent looking at computer screens or poring over research papers had left her body soft and rounded, and displaying the effects that gravity inevitably has on a woman over time unless hours are spent in the gym and pounds are spent on surgery. Ageing didn't bother Angela in the slightest. She had never suffered the curse of vanity and her interests were far more cerebral than physical, they always had been.

Her naturally grey hair was styled for practicality, short and neat. The only ornament to her face was a pair of red plastic rimmed glasses, that were often on the top of her head rather than in front of her eyes, making the hinges loose so that they often annoyingly slipped down her aquiline nose.

Angela had studied the crime scene photographs, the geographical locations of the crimes, the methodology of the killings and the characteristics of the victims.

She frowned often, but remained silent for quite some time before she finally spoke.

"I can't categorically say all three crimes were comitted by one person, particularly in the missing person case as the evidence is scant.

What I can say is that killers generally choose victims from within their own racial group so there is a likelihood he will be white. I say 'he' because of the strength needed to overpower these healthy, adult women. Also, statistically, these are likely to be the crimes of one killer rather than a pair or a group. This type of killer tends to be blue collar workers and the timing of the crimes supports this, evenings and late afternoons. Perhaps shift patterns?

The differences between the first and second killing indicate an escalation and a ritualistic element.

Removal of body parts in historical murders has been seen as trophy collecting or a sense if wanting to 'own' a victim, but this is predominantly in cases with a sexual motivation, such as Jeffery Dahmer, the American murderer.

There's no sexual motive here, but the removal of the eyes, tongue and hands are significant. He destroys the face of the second victim. That could well be indicative of great anger towards her or women in general. There's no real surgical skill though he could perhaps have basic knife skills from jointing food animals. Another thought I had was that these could be religiously significant.

'If thy eye offends thee, pluck it out, for it is better to enter the kingdom of God without sight, than be cast into hell with,' is vaguely the scripture, if my memory serves correctly. Similarly the tongue.

We use our tongue to speak, maybe he found her words offensive. The hands, symbolc perhaps of what we do. Did he find her actions offensive?

These are also indications of the possible mental state of the perpetrator. It would appear that his mental health is deteriorating although these appear to be organised rather than impulsive, disorganised crimes. The folding of the clothes, not a frantic bloodlust.

Religiosity is interestingly, a clinically recognised, mental disorder.

DI Johnson nodded. It made sense.

Angela continued," Geographically, if we draw lines to join the crime scenes we make a triangle. It is likely that our perpetrator lives within or near to the area of the triangle. You mentioned the driver's seat in the car of the missing woman. If the killer were the last person to drive this car, it would give him a minimum height of five foot ten, so a relatively tall individual.

The fact he was kneeling for enough time for blood to pool around his knees in the second killing indicates he is a fit man, definitely under fifty years. Kneeling becomes more difficult with age," she smiled knowingly at the two policeman.

"So, in conclusion, the perpetrator is likely to be a tall, white male, physically fit, under fifty and living and working in the locality. Something about these women offends him, possibly some religious aspect.

His crimes are escalating as his mental state is deteriorating. His killing is primarily organised in nature, he has selected his victims.

"We found a pentagram tattoo on Greta's body and we know Charlotte offered white witchcraft spells online," added Ian.

"The three Abrahamic faiths; Judaism, Islam, Christianity. All three warn against practising witchcraft," Angela told the policemen, "So, he could well believe he is fighting some kind of crusade or jihad, battling with the devil so to speak."

These are of course, based on statistics and probabilities. There is no cast iron guarantee that he will be exactly as I have described. These are merely indications."

After more questions from the two policemen, which Angela answered as well as she was able, she finished her now cold tea. DI Johnson thanked her for her time and expertise and DS Rasheed walked her through the station to the front door. It had started to rain. A pathetic drizzle, that looked set to continue for the rest of the afternoon judging by the iron grey colour of the heavy clouds above. Angela Hewson, put up her umbrella and, feeling decidedly hungry now, walked to a nearby cafe for a sandwich lunch and a decent cup of tea.

Chapter FortyEight. Closer.

Sarah frowned as she scrolled down the list of names. There were so many people who'd contacted Charlotte Redferne for help. She'd written down over a thousand different usernames.

She was raking it in, thought Sarah in astonishment as she read through the list of subscribers to Charlotte's Facebook page and YouTube channel.

She'd narrowed down the names to two lists. Those who had left positive comments and those who had left negative comments. Concentrating on the negative comments, comprised of non believing trolls, unsatisfied customers and those warning of dabbling in the dark arts. Jakub Kowalski was helping reverse search the senders. The ones in America and mainland Europe, Sarah thought they could discount for now for reasons of distance, but retained a list of their names for reference if needed.

Most of the trolls were harmless. A few were local, so she made a note of names and addresses.

Some of the disastisfied customers seemed very angry. There were a few threats. These would be quickly followed up.

The ones who sent warnings, were primarily from religious groups. The DI had told Sarah to keep a special eye out for any religious theme in the messages, so she made sure she included these. The remainder had watched one too many horror films in her opinion, but she included them anyway. She then listed this group in order of proximity, and they would start with the ones closest to Burnley. Trying each name through the criminal record programme, she looked for any previous convictions for violence. She also checked the electoral roll to see which names lived in the area that Professor Angela Hewson had marked on the map as being of interest.

It was satisfying seeing the long list of names getting gradually shorter. There was no guarantee Charlotte's murderer was even on the list but it was a line of enquiry that had to be explored thoroughly, and Sarah was going to make sure that it was.

She still felt guilty about Chris. Yes, he was an absolute knob, but he didn't deserve to be attacked so horribly. They still hadn't found the bearded hells angel or the blonde biker chick despite their appeals. Perhaps they were only travelling through the area and a national appeal was needed she wondered.

She kept thinking about the spell. Up until then, she'd only used magic for good, and she regretted the revenge spell, even though she still couldn't believe it could be that powerful. Sarah had thought he'd maybe find a girl who then dumped him, or break out in boils or something, but not lose an eye and be permanently disfigured.

She'd promised herself she would never use the dark side of magic again.

The list was gradually being whittled down.

She now wrote a new list of twelve names and their addresses, which she would pass on to DI Johnson in the morning.

Sarah's back now felt achey and stiff after hours spent hunched over the computer screen. She pushed back her chair and stretched her arms back over her head with a groan.

"Well, Kowalski," she said to her workmate in the next chair, "I'm off home for a hot shower, a glass of wine and an early night. Happy Halloween!"

"Ok, Sarah," he replied, "I've just got a bit more to do and then I'll be off home too, Happy Halloween to you too."

Sarah stood, and went to the DI's empty office, placing the list of names on his desk. Walking back through the main room, she waved a goodbye to Jakub and went to the locker room to gather her things for home.

Chapter FortyNine. Halloween

PC Sarah Preston drove home in her orange fiat, singing along to a Queens of the Stone Age song playing on the little car's radio. It was a running joke that as she was in the force, she needed a panda car, so that was exactly what she got, a fiat panda. She loved it. So easy to park and perfect for nipping around town. The bright orange paint job was not to everyone's taste, but it did make it easy to spot in supermarket car parks.

Sarah was a striking young woman, but not classically beautiful. Her eyes were narrowed and tilted giving them an oriental, catlike look which she emphasized with a sweep of black liquid eyeliner on each lid. Her lips were thin and overlined in a nude shade then filled in with a slightly lighter shade. On her days off she preferred red or deep purple shades, but these were frowned upon for work.

Arriving at her flat, she parked in her allotted space, pressed the door code numbers and entered the double height hallway. The lights came on automatically as they detected her movement.

After checking her postbox in the hall, she wearily climbed the stairs to her one bedroomed flat and unlocked the front door. Sarah's flat was one of six in an old, converted church. She loved the arched windows, quirky beams and stone work juxtapositioned with the modern glass panelled mezzanine balcony and high gloss kitchen units.

Throwing her coat over a high backed, steel grey, armchair and kicking her shoes underneath it, she sighed a tired sigh and sat on her black leather sofa, tossing the unopened mail next to her.

Looking at her phone, she saw a message from her friend, Maisie, asking what she would be wearing to their meeting that weekend. Sarah's thumbs speedily replied, 'Black maxi skirt and top. Taking a lush, velvet robe with a hood too x'

Scrolling down she found another message from an alternative clothing store informing her of a sale and another about an upcoming Halloween event at a local pub. She put both into her message trash. Then a message from her mother, asking her over for tea later in the week. She typed a quick reply, put her phone on to charge and then made her way to the modern bathroom.

A quick power shower later, she was wrapped in her white, towelling robe and wondering what to eat. Opening the freezer door, she looked hopefully through the drawers. Nothing excited her in there. Pizza it is then. Sarah ordered her usual double pepperoni on her phone app and then poured herself a large glass of red wine.

Lighting a white sage incense bundle, she placed it in an abalone shell holder on the high gloss black console table behind the sofa. The soothing scent began to gently drift through the room.

She then carried her wine to the black leather sofa, made herself comfortable and flicked on the tv whilst she waited for her food to arrive.

The buzzer sounded. That was quick, Sarah thought to herself but soon realised her mistake when she saw two short ghosts and a witch on the screen. Sarah smiled and went to get her tin of chocolates as she waited for the trick or treaters to climb the stairs to her door.

"Trick or treat," they shouted as Sarah opened the door with a look of mock fear, which quickly turned into a grin when she held out the open tin for the children to help themselves.

Shutting the door she settled back on the sofa.

The local news showed a smiling picture of Greta Gray, the murdered solicitor. She looked happy and far too young to be dead and gone. Still no leads. The tv journalist was appealing for information on behalf of the police. The camera cut to the designated press liason officer, who answered questions on the solicitor's last known movements.

It was scary thought Sarah, knowing that a killer was loose in her hometown and there were no obvious leads. At least she was safely locked in her little flat with top spec cctv in the communal hallway.

The buzzer sounded again. This time it was her pizza and she pressed the door release to let him in. She sipped her wine as she watched the rest of the news programme before pouring one last glass and searching through the channels for a good movie. She found an interesting looking thriller and curled her feet under her as she settled down to watch it.

The buzzer sounded and Sarah got up. After checking the tiny screen, and seeing the pizza delivery man, she pressed the enter button. She was starving. Peeping through the peephole in her flat doorway, she saw him appear at the top of her stairs with his familiar cycle helmet.

She opened the door with a smile and took the pizza from him with a quick, "Thank you," before shutting the door.

Almost immediately the buzzer sounded again. The little screen showed a frankenstein mask. Sarah pressed the enter button again and smiling, grabbed the tin of chocolates. A gentle knock on the door. She opened wide the door with a smile which instantly disappeared as she felt the hard punch to her face. Staggering backwards and then falling onto her back, scattering chocolates everywhere, a look of puzzlement appeared on Sarah's face. The masked man knelt over her prone body, put his hands firmly around her neck and began to strangle her. She tried to claw at his fingers to loosen his grip but the leather motorcycle gloves meant she couldn't do him any damage. She just painfully bent back her long nails. She kicked with her bare legs but he was just too strong. Writhing underneath him, she was desperate for oxygen and panicking now. Losing control of her bladder, a stream of warm urine yellowed the back of her white, towelling robe. She fought with the little strength she had left but it was no use. She tried to scream but her throat was too constricted. Rapidly losing conciousness, her struggling lessened and finally stopped.

The attacker stood and walked to the kitchen and took a large, carving knife out of the wooden knife block. He walked calmly back to the unconcious policewoman and forcefully stabbed the knife into her pale throat, sawing with a ragged motion across her exposed neck severing both the jugular vein and the carotid artery. The pain and adrenaline flowing through her bloodstream shocked her back in to conciousness and her green eyes grew wide in helpless fear. A few rasping breaths accompanied by a bloody bubbling from the jagged wound finally signalled the end of Sarah Preston. The attacker waited for her to still, then began carving into Sarah as if she were a Halloween pumpkin.

When he was finished, he rinsed off the blood before he left the flat, closing the door gently behind him.

Sarah Preston lay motionless, her blood slowly coagulating and seeping into the cream, wool carpet. The flickering light of the tv screen reflecting off her lifeless eyes.

Chapter Fifty. News.

It was the first of November, All Hallows.

There was a feeling of fear in the town. Three murders now meant a serial killer was in their midst. The papers were having a field day, calling him the 'Burnley Strangler'. Three gruesome murders in such a short space of time. Speculation was rife about who he was, and why he was killing people. In some cases, family members were eyeing each other with suspicion.

The nationals had got hold of the story and tv. crews had been seen in the town.

Ian had put Ishmael Patel in charge of press releases. Today, Ishmael had called a press conference where reporters from tv and newspapers could put their questions to DI Johnson.

They were setting up the hall now. There was a podium, with around a dozen microphones attached to it of differing colours, shapes and sizes. Lighting rigs were being assembled at each side and a pull down screen with the Lancashire constabulary badge in the centre provided a back drop.

Ishmael and Ian were in the detectives office discussing which were the essential details they needed out there in the public domain and which to hold back. Also, they wanted to allay the fears of the general public whilst keeping them safe and alert for any activity or individuals that could aid them in solving the crimes. It was a fine balancing act.

"Ok, let's get this done," said Ian determinedly as he stood and walked with Ishmael to the large hall that was usually used for briefings and training.

As soon as the two men appeared, cameras began to flash. Ishmael began by telling the reporters that DI Johnson would explain the case first and that they should wait until the end of his presentation, when there would be an opportunity to ask questions. Ishmael then stepped back and Ian stepped up to the podium. On a stand to his right were pictures of Greta Grey, Charlotte Redferne and Sarah Preston on a large whiteboard screen.

DI Johnson began to speak,

"Good evening. My name is Inspector Ian Johnson, I am the detective charged with the investigation into the deaths of three women, Greta Grey, Charlotte Redferne and Police Constable Sarah Preston.

Three young women with their futures cruelly snatched away. We have cctv footage of Ms. Grey leaving the gym on St. Peter's Street at 8pm on Friday the twenty seventh of September this year. As you can see, Ms. Grey is seen, jogging towards the car park, " Ian used a laser pointer to indicate Greta's position on the screen," We then lose contact with her as she enters the car park itself. This is the last time we have a sighting of Ms. Grey, and we believe she was killed soon afterwards."

Ian clicked to change the screen. Now a video of Charlotte Redferne appeared taken from her Facebook page.

Mrs. Redferne was killed sometime between twelve and three on the afternoon of Friday October the eighteenth.

" Mrs. Redferne was a wife and a mother of two young children. She had an active life on social media and this is the last video that she recorded before she was killed in her own home," He played a portion of the video for the reporters.

"We are currently working our way through the people who contacted Mrs. Redferne via social media.

The latest victim is Sarah Preston. As you can no doubt imagine, the officers working on this case are understandably upset by the death of a dear friend and colleague."

He clicked to show cctv footage from Sarah's flat.

"The last sighting of Ms. Preston was on the evening of Wednesday the 31st of October as she entered her building. It was Halloween so there were quite a number of trick or treaters out that night. We are keen to find this man," Ian clicked to a grainy still from the cctv. As you can see, his face is covered by the bike helmet, but he is carrying what looks to be a pizza box. We estimate him to be around five foot ten in height, slim build. We have no record of which pizza company was delivering as Ms. Preston's phone has not been found and we suspect her attacker may have taken it with him. We have no cctv of the bike he was using.

We are also extremely concerned for the welfare of Cheryl Hargraves, 48, who has been missing since early October.

Back at home, Eve sat on the gold velvet sofa watching the tv. She knew her husband would be on this evenings news and was keen to know how the press conference went.

"Good Evening, It's Friday the first of November, I'm Anna Stokes and here are today's headlines." said the polished voice. After listing the main stories of the day, the newsreader moved on to the lead story. She spoke about the upcoming general election and Nigel Ferage's Brexit speech and something about Boris Johnson's latest faux pas before introducing the story of the murders and cutting to the tape of Ian's press conference saying, "A warning, there is flash photography from the beginning of this report."

As she watched her husband explaining the last known movements of the three victims, tears fell from her eyes and she hugged one of the teal cushions tightly. It was just too horrible seeing the faces of those women, knowing what had happened to them. She couldn't begin to imagine how she would feel if anything like that ever happened to Yasmin or Joel. She shivered involuntarily and when the report was finished, went to pour herself a calming glass of wine.

Chapter FiftyOne. Bonfire.

It was a cold fifth of November, with a clear, obsidian black sky. Thank goodness it wasn't raining, thought Janet as she wrapped up the two children, in coats, woolly hats, mittens and wellies, ready to go out. It was always a bit of a weather lottery on bonfire night. Heavy showers could, quite literally, make the event a bit of a damp squib. Tonight though, the weather gods were smiling on them, as it was the perfect night to watch a display.

Darren had previously bought a family ticket for the community fireworks event at Towneley park, and was coming to pick them all up in his car.

Hearing the beep of a horn, Janet ushered the children outside to the waiting car. Darren grinned at Harry and Amy, "Alright you two, ready to see the fireworks?"

The children raised their little arms, "Yay!"

Two year old Amy didn't really know what fireworks were, but she picked up on her elder brother's excitement and knew it was something to look forward to.

Janet strapped the children into their respective car seats before walking around to the passenger door, getting in and exchanging a kiss with Darren.

"Oooo, your nose is cold!" he said, feigning a shiver.

"You're lucky it didn't drip on you!" she laughed, "It's brass monkeys tonight."

They drove excitedly the short journey to the car park, before tumbling out of the car and walking into the park itself. Out in the open, there was a slight breeze, but not enough to affect the display.

Wandering around the muddy fields were lots of other families and couples out to watch the fireworks. The sound of chatter and laughter filled the air, and there was an atmosphere of excited anticipation. Most, at least the foresighted ones, were in wellingtons or stout boots, others were regretting their choice of white trainers or slip on shoes as they began to experience the wet kind of cold that only comes from wearing soggy socks.

There were fairground rides, a burger van, a converted campervan selling gourmet hot chocolate, a balloon seller and a small marquee style tent containing chairs, tables, crayons and bonfire night colouring pages to keep everyone occupied until the actual display. The bonfire was already lit and they could feel the warmth even far outside the barriers around it.

Finding a brightly painted roundabout lit with dozens of warm yellow bulbs, they let the children choose what to ride on. There was a bright red, double decker bus, a horse with a golden mane, an old fashioned yellow car with a horn you could squeeze, a blue painted dolphin splashing in a painted sea, a giraffe with big, cartoon eyes and a green motorbike with side car.

Both children went to sit on the red bus.

As the roundabout turned accompanied by traditional fairground music, the children laughed and waved out of the cutout bus windows. Janet took more photos as they rode the bus around and around until eventually, the ride slowed down and it was time to get off.

Next, all four of them tried to hook a duck to win a prize. The children received a little help from the adults and managed to win a bouncy ball and tub of bubbles, which Janet put in her bag for later. Wandering around the stalls, Janet felt content. She felt they were becoming a real, happy family. Leaning over, she planted a kiss of Darren's cheek which made him smile.

"Train!" shouted Harry, pointing to another roundabout. This one was comprised of an old fashioned steam train engine and four carriages. They all went on this ride together, with Harry pretending he was driving the train and pulling on a rope that swung a brass bell. Darren leaned over to Janet and quietly whispered, "I love you."

Janet smiled and answered the same. They kissed as the little train went round in circles until the ride finally came to a stop.

Holding hands with each other and one child each, they leisurely walked some more until they arrived at the burger van. The smell was incredible, frying onions mingled with beef, and they ordered four cheeseburgers. There's something about a cheeseburger, wrapped in a serviette, from a greasy van, eaten outside in the cold, that makes it taste that little bit extra. Hot, and calorific, with sauce dripping down their chins, they enjoyed the burgers just as much as they would a five star hotel dinner.

It was time for the display. Still chewing mouthfuls of cheeseburger they gazed in to the sky as scores of multi coloured, sparkling rockets exploded into expanding, shimmering circles of kaleidoscopic light. Following those, came fireworks that rose in bright, white spirals high into the black, night sky and screamed throughout their journey. Amy held her mittened hands over her ears at the loud wails, as she laughed with the pure joy only a child knows.

Children stared, wide eyed, upwards in amazement, the fireworks reflected in their shiny eyes.

Darren's arm slipped around Janet's waist as they looked up into the beautiful night sky, and Janet felt happy. Really happy.

A row of golden fountains of fine, glitter-like sparkles were followed by rockets that exploded with a bang, high in the sky into globules of lava-red light.

A blizzard of white erupted into a snow storm of pure light that looked beautiful in its simplicity, and finally a fast, explosive round of rockets in purples and greens, bursting one after the other in rapid fire showering the sky in brightly coloured rain.

Cordite scented smoke swirled around the crowd as they clapped in appreciation of the fantastic display.

Janet, Darren and the two children walked happily back to his car and Darren smiled as he thought to himself, there was nowhere he would rather be.

Chapter FiftyTwo. Approval.

The sun was low but bright. So low, the visors at the top of the windscreen were not deep enough to block out the glare as they drove to Janet's grandma's. Darren screwed up his eyes against the brightness.

The journey took them up a steep hill, through an old council estate that had been built in the fifties. Most of the houses were now privately owned through the 'right to buy,' scheme introduced in the nineties, but some still housed council tenants like Janet's grandma. Janet looked out of the window as she chatted to Darren whilst Harry and Amy sat in their car seats, enjoying the ride.

The little old car finally reached their destination, and Darren parked on the street. Janet stepped out of the car and unbuckled the children. Darren opened the boot and took out a bunch of chrysanthemums, lillies and roses in shade of lemon and cream.

He knocked on the pvc door to the little, pebble-dashed, bungalow. Janet stood next to him holding Amy on her hip with Harry holding onto her hand.

Grandma Shauna opened the door with a broad smile on her face, "Come in, come in, afore you let all the heat out."

Shauna led the little family into her small living room. She had lived on her own in the bungalow since her husband, Patrick, had died over a decade ago.

"Sit yourselves down," she instructed as she brought out a basket of toys and placed it on the thick, rust coloured rug in front of the sofa. "It's a cold one today, so it is. Take your coats off now, or you won't feel the benefit when you leave, " advised Shauna, "I'll go put the kettle on."

Shauna disappeared into her little kitchen, making tea and cutting up fruit cake.

Darren looked around the tiny living room. An old wooden wall unit covered one wall. It's shelves holding various china ornaments and a selection of romance novels. The carpet was patterned with beige fleur-de-lis on a red background and deep red, velvet curtains hung at the window.

Shauna returned with a plastic tray carrying the cake, a teapot, milk jug, sugar basin and three cups and saucers. Placing the tray on a kidney shaped side table, she began to pour the tea.

"Now then," she said as she finally sat down in her red, velvet chair, "What's new in the world?"

"Amy has another tooth," said Janet.

"Aww, that's grand. She'll be grown afore you know it, so she will," replied Shauna, "And how about you young man? What's the craic with yourself?"

"Am doing ok. Had that bad cold that was going around, but I'm feeling a lot better now," answered Darren.

"Ah. Janet told me you had a bad dose," continued Shauna, "Had it meself so I did, sweet baby Jesus, brutal so it was. What about these murders eh? Whoever it is is not the full shillin'. Make sure you look after my grandaughter, fella, with that eejit on the loose."

"I will," Darren replied reassuringly, "Janet is very important to me."

"Never used to be like this," said Shauna, "Donkey's years ago, you used to be able to leave your doors unlocked all day, night too if you were so inclined, no problem, but now?" she made a face as though she'd smelled something bad, "The oul fella, God rest his soul, would be turnin' in his grave at all these shenanigans. But it's the times. Mary, mother o' God. Young 'uns growin' up with not an ounce of respect fer people or fer things. They need to get tough on the buggers, the oul fell woulda kicked ten shades out of anyone taking the feckin' Michael like these young uns do."

" I did warn Darren you could talk the hind legs off a donkey, gran," laughed Janet, then turning to Darren said," Never mind kissing the Blarney stone, I think gran must have swallowed the fecker! "

Shauna let out a crackling, mucousy raucous laugh, " Ahh, you do brighten my day, so you do Janet, " she said wiping a tear from her eye.

Darren grinned broadly, enjoying the quirky nature of the conversation.

They continued drinking tea, eating cake and putting the world to rights as the children happily played on the rug, until it was time to go.

Darren was helping Harry zip up his coat as Shauna looked out of the window, "Aw b'Jaysus, it's bucketing it down!" she warned the young couple, "Watch how you go, mind."

At the door, Shauna caught hold of Darren's arm, "You'll do," she said approvingly. Darren smiled back at the old woman.

The rain was sheeting it down as they ran to the car, making streams of the gutters. Once inside and strapped in, Darren started the engine and put the windscreen wipers on the maximum setting. "Bye now," called Shauna as the little, old car set off in the pouring rain to Janet's house with little hands waving goodbye at the windows.

"I think she likes you," Janet said teasingly.

"Don't they all?" replied Darren and Janet gave him a playful punch on the arm.

Chapter FiftyThree. Fade.

The wind ripped at the loose corner of the poster as it curled around the lamp post until it eventually tore. In fact, most of the posters from which the permanently smiling face of Cheryl Hargraves looked out were beginning to look a little dogeared and old. They were widespread over the town and Cheryl was probably the most famous person in Burnley at that moment.

The same picture had been shared countless times over social media and even on the local news. There had been a few reported sightings. Someone had phoned to say that she'd been seen in a fish and chip restaurant in Cleveleys, another that she was working in the B & Q in Burnley, and another still swore blind they'd seen her in the audience of Strictly Come Dancing as they watched tv one Saturday evening. None bore fruit and Cheryl was still missing.

At the warehouse, a collection had been made but up until now, it just sat in a jar as they were unsure exactly what to do with it.

As time went by, the possibility that Cheryl might never be found grew stronger. In small ways a Cheryl free way of life crept up on them. A new woman sat in Cheryl's chair tapping away at her keyboard. On a temporary contract of course, the bosses weren't quite that insensitive. Her name was Tracee, with an 'ee' not a 'y'. The warehouse team couldn't quite take to her though. She just wasn't Cheryl. It felt disloyal somehow, so there were no jokes cracked around the office or cheeky banter. People just came in, collected orders and left again. Luckily, Tracee with an 'ee' didn't seem to mind and just got on with the job.

The workmates asked Mohammed less frequently now if there was any news of Cheryl. It seemed repetitive after a while and the answer was always the same. Laughter began to be heard again in the warehouse. Her name wasn't even on the list for the Christmas do.

It was as though Cheryl, or the memory of her, was slowly dissolving away, like sugar in hot tea. Disappating, until there was nothing left, but a taste of the sweetness.

Darren was taping up order twelve.

"Thought I'd actually cook for you this weekend, are you up for it?" he asked Janet.

"Sure! I'll ask my grandma if she can have the kids," she answered smiling as she peeled off a label and stuck it on the box of her tenth order.

Tariq was on his fourteenth order. Janet knew he'd make a good picker and packer, she spotted that from early on. She would put a tenner on him being made permanent by Christmas.

Mohammed was having a quiet word with Liam. He'd noticed Liam's work rate was slowing a little of late and he didn't always smell very fresh. Mohammed obviously knew that Liam had lost his mother recently and had made allowances but now wondered if he was finding living alone difficult or suffering from depression.

"Liam, how are things with you?" Mohammed began.

"Fine," answered Liam, a little too quickly, "Why you ask this?"

Mohammed licked his lips, "Well, I know your mother died and that's always hard. I just wondered. You know, me and Nasreen would love you to come round for something to eat one night. Your place must seem a bit quiet at times."

Liam looked surprised, he wasn't expecting an invitation to dinner. He was silent for a moment, wondering how to respond, then accepted Mohammed's offer, shaking his hand,"Thank you Mo, it's very kind of you. That would be good, my friend."

" Ok, good, good," said Mohammed, "Shall we say Thursday?"

Liam nodded and smiled warmly.

"I'll let Nasreen know," said Mohammed, walking away to phone his wife as he spoke. Nasreen was absolutely fine about the news of a guest for dinner on Thursday. She loved cooking and felt as part of her muslim faith, she should practise hospitality. "I'll make that Persian lamb dish, it's fairly mild but very tasty. Oh, and could you pick up a box of Asian sweets from Mansha?"

"Yes, of course Nasreen," said her husband.

"Oh," she remembered another thing, "Pomegranates, can you pick a couple up for me please, mérè patì?"

"Jee, I'll stop off on the way home méra mi□hú," Mohammed said.

Nasreen thanked him before saying good bye, "Sukara hai, baí,"

As he was reading through his next order sheet, Liam was thinking about the invitation. It had certainly surprised him, but he thought that it did fit with Mo's caring nature. Mo was a good manager who took the responsibility of the role seriously.

He wasn't sure at all what answer to give to Mo's invitation that would be for the best, but in the end, he thought he would use the example of Jesus, who went to eat with sinners. Mo wasn't evil as such, just misled by false religion thought Liam. Maybe he could show Mohammed the way.

Chapter FiftyFour. Lamb.

Nasreen had spent all afternoon cooking. The whole house smelled of onions and spices.

She'd laid a royal blue tablecloth embroidered with an intricate floral design in metallic gold thread on the large dining table. Blue floating candles and lotus blossoms sat in a wide glass bowl of water in the centre.

Nasreen wore a royal blue tunic with gold embroidery detailing at the neck and three quarter cuffs and plain black trousers. She didn't cover her hair as many did these days, trying to be ultra religious, to wear every badge of Islam they could to show the world they were muslim. She wasn't brought up to cover her head, her husband had never commented, but most importantly, she held Islam in her heart. Allah knew that and that was enough for her.

Nasreen filled a jug with ice and poured in a carton of mango juice and a few mint leaves.

Mohammed opened the door to his home and immediately smelled the aroma of his wife's cooking. Liam followed him inside.

"Ah, welcome home, and welcome to you too Liam. It's good to meet one of my husband's workmates," Nasreen said warmly, " "Thank you for inviting me," said Liam, "It's very kind of you. Your husband is a good man."

Nasreen looked proudly at her husband. He was indeed, she thought to herself. She poured the chilled mango juice into glasses and handed them to Mohammed and Liam, "Please, sit. I've just a couple if things to finish up in the kitchen so if you'll excuse me, you two men talk among yourselves."

Back in the kitchen, Nasreen cut up red onion, a red chilli and coriander leaves for a salad. As she juiced a lemon, she listened to the two men talking away next door. Busying herself frying the chicken pakora, she could no longer hear them above the bubbling of the hot oil.

She set a piece of kitchen roll on a plate to absorb and surplus grease before putting the pakora in a fresh dish to serve, sprinking chopped coriander leaves on top.

She carried the pakora, a tomato salad, raita and the onion salad into the dining room, placing them on the table, with serving spoons. "Please, come eat," Nasreen said, inviting the men to the table, "Will you eat the traditional way or would you like a knife and fork?"

"I will eat as you eat," replied Liam as he sat down.

Nasreen sat briefly with the men, making conversation, but soon disappeared back into the kitchen.

"So Liam, how are you finding things now your mother has passed. It must feel take some getting used to," asked Mohammed.

Liam swallowed his mouthful of chicken, washing it down with a mouthful of juice before speaking.

"It is different Mo. I've closed off her room. It's better that way," he explained, "Fresh start."

Mohammed nodded, "You must miss her."

"No," said Liam flatly, "She lived her life how she chose. Now she's moved on. Gone to the next life. I remain. I have to live my life, you know Mo?"

Mohammed frowned. It might just be the language barrier, but Liam didn't sound right.

Nasreen appeared with the persian lamb, a dish that used to be reserved for weddings in her family. She placed the serving dish on the table, before removing the pakora plates. Returning, she set fresh plates down and brought in the roti and fragrant rice.

"It smells good!" said Liam, "Your wife is a good cook Mo. You are a lucky man."

Nasreen smiled at the compliment before replying, "I am very lucky too."

Spooning the food onto his plate, Liam was glad he'd accepted the invitation.

He tasted the lamb. "Mmm, the Lamb of God, who takes away the sins of the world."

Mohammed exchanged a glance with his wife, puzzled by Liam's words, but Liam just kept his eyes down, scooping up lamb in his folded roti and stuffing it greedily into his mouth.

"You know, Mo," he said as he wiped up the last of the sauce with a piece of roti then put it in his mouth. Nasreen picked up their empty plates and returned to the kitchen. He chewed and swallowed before continuing,

"Mo. I need to tell you because you are a good friend to Liam." Mohammed noticed the switch of Liam's speech into the third person.

"Mo. You," he jabbed his finger towards his friend, "Are going to hell. Hell. But Liam can save you."

Mohammed pushed back his chair and went to stand, but Liam put his hands on Mohammed's shoulders.

"This is important Mo. They named you after a false prophet. Trust Liam."

Mohammed stood up, despite Liam's grip, unsure whether to feel anger or pity. Luckily his wife walked back into the room before anger won. She looked confused, then frightened.

"You can't insult the prophet in my home Liam. Please don't say things like that."

"He wasn't a prophet," said Liam, "Theyare lying to you!"

"Who is lying to me Liam. You're not making any sense?"

Liam looked at Mohammed with pity, then spoke with a low, serious voice, "The demons."

"Liam, it's time to go," Mohammed said in a measured tone.

"Ok, sure," said Liam holding up his open palms, "Pearls before swine. Liam understands, but he gave you a chance. If they don't listen, shake the dust from your shoes and leave. Bye my friend." With that, Liam left Mohammed and Nasreen's house, and went home, totally oblivious to the offence he had caused.

"Nasreen, I'm so sorry," her husband said sadly, "He really isn't well." Mohammed pointed at his skull as he said the word 'well.' "We will keep him in our prayers," Nasreen replied, "You did your best. It's all Insha' Allah now. Remember, the mercy of Allah is greater than any sin."
They held each other, each grateful they had the other. As for Liam, what did he have? Mohammed would certainly pray for Allah's mercy and healing.

Chapter FiftyFive.
Religiosity.

It was a bright, clear morning. It had rained in the night and a steamy mist rose up from the wet tarmac of the road as it was warmed by the first rays of the white, winter sun. Mohammed kissed his wife goodbye and got into his pillar box red, vauxhall astra. He'd been worrying last night and again this morning about Liam's behaviour over dinner.
He pulled down the visor to shade his eyes from the blindingly low sun. As he drove, his mind was going over and over what was said and how to deal with it this morning. It was beyond rude, there was definitely something wrong mentally with Liam. He had seemed agitated, detached somehow and not at all his usual self. Talking about himself in the third person was definitely not normal.
Part of Mohammed was dreading the conversation he would need to have with Liam. Mohammed was a kind, gentle man. He could be strong when needed, but found it less comfortable.
Arriving at work, Mohammed parked in his usual place, noticing that Liam's old motorbike had not yet arrived. Entering the office, he said

a quick hello to Tracee with an 'ee,' before walking through the warehouse to the staffroom to make a brew.

As the kettle boiled, he practised in his head, how the conversation would go. As the kettle clicked he was snapped out of his train of thought and made himself a mug of hot, sweet tea. Sitting down at a table in the empty staffroom he drank his tea and mused further on the situation.

Tariq entered the room and filled a glass with tap water. "Alright Mo," he said as he sat in the seat opposite Mohammed, placing his glass on the formica tabletop.

"Not too great this morning Tariq," admitted the older man, "How are you finding things?"

"Am good," replied Tariq.

Mohammed asked a further question, "Getting on ok with everyone?"

Tariq thought for a momeny, "Yes, I think so, Liam's being a bit weird though," he replied.

"How so?" asked Mohammed sitting up a little straighter.

Tariq swallowed, "He was ok at first, a bit quiet but I don't mind that. Recently he's been going on and on about Islam and how I should 'turn to the truth'."

The older man nodded. This was what he'd been afraid of, but it did also give him leverage in speaking to Liam. Religious discrimination laws in the workplace had been introduced in the mid nineties, and he knew Liam's behaviour would be viewed as such by the bosses. Liam was getting to be a serious problem.

"I'll have a word," Mohammed reassured Tariq, "You shouldn't have to put up with that at work. Is he in yet?"

"I don't think so, unless he's arrived as I've been in here," said Tariq.

"There's still a couple of minutes until it's time," said Mohammed looking at his watch, "You're well thought of here and doing a good job. As soon as he's in, I'll have a chat."

Tariq drained his glass, "Thanks Mo," he said smiling, "I best go crack on."

The young man stood and went to collect his orders from the office.

Sighing, Mohammed got up taking Tariq's glass along with his own mug to the sink before going for his own orders.

Fifteen minutes later, there was still no sign of Liam in the warehouse. After half an hour, Mohammed went to ask at the office if he had rung in sick. Tracee shook her head, "No one's phoned in sick today."

Frowning to himself, Mohammed decided he would leave it a little longer before he would ring Liam himself.

Back at his flat, Liam sat naked in his old, green armchair. He'd sat there all night. The scritch, scratch, scritch of Cheryl's fingernails had robbed him of any sleep, so he'd got up, and sat quietly in his chair, staring at the wall.

The curtains were still closed despite the hour and the room was gloomy and dark, full of shadows. Liam listened. He heard something. The Holy Spirit was speaking to him through the wind. It was louder than the scratching. He heard it more clearly now and listened with an urgency. With wide eyes, he rocked backwards and forwards as he listened, nodding at times.

His phone rang at one point, breaking his concentration, but Liam waited for it to stop ringing and then switched it off, and resumed his listening. He wanted no distractions as the Spirit gave him instructions about his calling.

Goosebumps covered his arms and legs but he couldn't feel the cold. He had fire in his veins. He didn't even need to eat. Jesus spent forty days without food in the wilderness. The Spirit would nourish him.

"But I say unto you, I will not drink henceforth of this fruit of the vine until that day I drink it anew with you in my Father's Kingdom. Liam will follow the example of Christ. He will pick up his cross and do the bidding of Almighty God," said Liam, voicing aloud his vow, as Jesus had at the last supper. He would not listen to the weakness of his flesh he thought as he rocked to and fro in the darkness.

Long after the unseen sun had slipped silently behind the hills, Liam stood, knowing what he now had to do. Dressing quickly, he made the necessary preparations to fulfil his spiritual mission.

Chapter FiftySix. Transition.

It was a Monday. Liam had completed his daily run up Pendle Hill and was now in Towneley Park. It was the eleventh day of the eleventh month. The day when those killed in conflict are gratefully remembered by those whose freedom they died fighting for.

Close to Towneley Hall, was a small, hidden away garden area with a magnificent, memorial to fallen soldiers, sailors and airmen. Three carved servicemen, one from each of the armed forces, rise solemnly out of the solid stone, upon which an inscription, remembering the Burnley folk, who gave their lives in two great wars, is carved. The warriors are flanked by two bronze female figures, representing the womenfolk who never got to see their son, husband or sweetheart return.

Poppy wreaths had been laid at the base of the memorial, in a respectful ceremony attended by the mayor of Burnley. It was a hundred years since the Great War of 1914 finally ended after four long years of pain, suffering and sacrifice.

Liam felt the importance of the date. After the ceremony had finished, and he stood alone, before the cenotaph, looking upwards into the faces of those stone figures, he felt a strange affinity. He himself was a soldier, fighting the good fight, a one man crusade against evil forces who conspired with machiavellian wickedness to destroy the peace of his town.

Another great event made this day significant. Today, the planet Mercury would transition the sun, which according to astrologists, would mean a rebirth into a stronger, higher level of conciouness.

Mercury being the planet of communication, calls for a greater self awareness and connection with the universe.

Burnley gentleman and astronomer, Richard Towneley, of the famous Towneley family that once lived in the Hall itself, saw the transition of Mercury three hundred years ago.

Numerology also elevates the number eleven as a Master number, associated with spiritual awakenings and higher powers.

This day, this very day, was a day to absorb all the energy from these significant events. Liam closed his eyes as he raised his hands to the heavens.

"Fill me, oh Lord," he cried out into the air.

He felt the universe answer, like lava flowing slowly through every inch of his body. He felt empowered and strengthened. Sinking to his knees in thanks and worship, eyes remaining closed and head tipped back, Liam laughed out loud, immersing himself in the experience, feeling the power of the Almighty at work in him.

Listening for the words of his Master, Liam went silent. He waited, and eventually he heard it,

"My son, in whom I am well pleased."

Tears fell from Liam's eyes at this supreme honour bestowed upon him.

Chapter FiftySeven.
Lasagne.

It was the twelth of November. Janet put down her knife and fork on the empty plate and sighed.

"So you can cook after all!" she said, smiling at Darren, "That was really good."

Darren grinned and picked up her plate,

"I must confess, I do make a mean lasagne. "

They were at Darren's house as Janet's children were sleeping over at their great grandma's house again.

He took the plates into the kitchen and returned with the remainder of the red wine he'd bought to go with dinner.

"Top up?" he asked and Janet lifted up her glass. Refreshing her drink, Darren asked if she wanted ice-cream.

"I couldn't eat another thing," Janet replied, "Am stuffed."

After emptying the rest of the wine into his own glass, Darren sat down next to Janet.

"Cheers," he said, and the pair clinked glasses and sipped their wine.

The couple locked eyes and smiled. "Do you know, Janet Brown, I think I might be falling in love with you."

Janet smiled, "Well Darren Hewitt, I may just be falling in love with you too."

Darren took her glass and placed it on the black glass side table, next to his own. He then took her face in both hands and gently kissed her soft lips. They gazed longingly into each others eyes.

His voice hoarse, Darren said, "You go up, I'll just lock up and then I'll be right behind you."

Janet smiled and climbed the stairs to the bathroom as Darren tidied away the glasses.

As he was coming back through the hall, Darren heard a knock on the front door. Puzzled he opened the door. Immediately a fist punched him square in the face, hard, sending him sprawling onto his back, dazed.

Janet stopped brushing her teeth and listened. She heard the front door slam shut and Darren's voice shouting, "What the fuck?" before hearing another thud.

Her eyes widened in fear and she fumbled for her phone. She was shaking as she pressed 999. After two rings the operator answered and Janet whispered into the phone.

Downstairs, Darren was fighting for his life, but his attacker was stronger, taller and determined. The taller man tried to get his hands around Darren's neck, but Darren squirmed and wriggled, clawing with his hands, preventing him getting a proper grip.

Changing tactics, the attacker pulled back his arm and punched Darren hard in the face. The younger man's nose exploded, spattering blood and mucous across his face and then the world went black as he lost conciousness.

After a few moments, Darren began to come around, awakened by the sounds of metal grating against metal. He gradually opened his eyes. The taller man was searching the cutlery drawer in the kitchen. Darren tried to rise to a sitting position, but the pain stopped him, he winced and white dots of light circled around his closed eyelids.

The attacker had found what he wanted, a large carving knife and he returned to Darren, still lying on the floor. Janet watched horrified as the hooded man knelt over her boyfriend and raised the knife.

Janet crept silently down the stairs and now swung the dumbell she had found upstairs, hard on the back of the head of Darren's attacker. The noise was a sickening thud, metal on flesh and bone. He slumped and fell across her boyfriend. Darren kicked and squirmed his way out from underneath and Janet went to hold him. Hugging Darren tightly to her she became aware of blue lights and the noise of sirens and suddenly the door burst open, and five police officers burst into the narrow hallway, shouting warnings. Tears of relief sprang from Janet's eyes and she began to sob as she shook uncontrollably on the floor. A police officer was placing handcuffs on the still unconcious attacker as paramedics entered the little house.

"Are you hurt," a female paramedic asked and Janet shook her head. She the medic turned her attention to Darren and a male paramedic knelt beside the unconcious attacker.

DI Johnson entered the hallway and crouched down on his haunches next to the attacker. The paramedic was checking the attacker's vital signs. Janet couldn't see the attackers prone body past the kneeling group of professionals tending to the two men and she was thankful for the distance.

Chapter FiftyEight.
Interview.

Liam sat on a grey, plastic chair at a grey table in the grey, interview room at the station. He wore a bandage round his head covering the spot where Janet had hit him with the dumbell, but he'd been discharged from hospital after a night of observation. No concussion, just a small laceration where it glanced off his scalp. DI Johnson entered the room with DS Rasheed and the two policemen sat on similar grey chairs. Plastic bottles of water sat on the formica tabletop.

DS Rasheed started the tape. He cleared his throught and began, "For the benefit of the tape, the time is" (he looked at his wristwatch) "approximately 1.15am, Thursday, 31st October, 2019. Present in the room are myself, Detective Sargent Abdul Rasheed and Detective Inspector Ian Johnson.

For the benefit if the tape could you please state your name and date of birth."

"Liam Horvat. 01.01.91,"

"Mr. Horvat, or can I call you Liam?" began DI Johnson.

"Liam is fine," he replied in his thick accent.

"Thank you," Ian continued, " Liam, I know English is not your first language, you can request an interpreter."

Liam shook his head.

"For the benefit of the tape, could you please answer the question verbally. Would you like an interpreter?"

"No," said Liam emphatically.

Johnson continued, "Liam, you have been arrested on suspicion of a very grave offence, but I believe you have refused a solicitor. I think under the circumstances, and it being your right under U. K. law, I would recommend you appoint a solicitor or we could find one for you"

"No," replied, "I don't need a solicitor. You wouldn't understand," said Liam making a dismissive motion with his hand.

DI Johnson nodded, "OK. Then can you help me understand?"

Liam leaned forward, his forearms resting on the table,speaking in a conspiratorial tone, "Witchcraft. It's an evil curse on this land" he said.

The two detectives listened.

"Witchcraft?," said Johnson, "Why is that so important to you, Liam?"

"You had your own witches, here, in Lancashire, yes? The Pendle witches? I've studied their stories, the trial, the executions. We have witchcraft in my country. Vlack magic. My mother was Vlach. She did not know any better but she married my father. He taught her about the true faith."

DS Rasheed nodded, wondering where exactly this was going.

Liam continued," They killed my father. Shot him. He refused to convert in the war. We were so scared. I was maybe five when he died. A small boy. Then there were the guns, the bombs, the soldiers. It was hell on earth. People who were once neighbours became enemies. Terrible times, terrible," Liam shook his head thinking back to his past.

" My mother. She was never the same after that. Neither was I. They called it PTSD, but I wasn't ill like they said. I was a boy. It is normal to be scared of evil, no? " said Liam, seeking some validation and agreement from the policemen.

Johnson nodded," In that situation, I would be scared, definitely. "

" It's natural, yes? " Liam continued," The bombs, the noise of the guns, the dead bodies piled by the side of the road as we walked and walked. It was so very cold. Very cold. I thought I would die from the cold alone! But we survived. I prayed to God and he saved us. I said then. I told my mother, my life is for God. He will protect us and I will serve Him all my life. And I have."

"How does that relate to your attack on Mr. Hewitt?" asked DS Rasheed.

Liam sighed as though he were explaining to some dull witted child, "Darren Hewitt. You don't recognise the surname?"

The two policemen exchanged glances.

"No," replied DI Johnson, "should we?"

"Of course!" exclaimed Liam with a touch of exasperation in his voice, "It's your history, not mine! Hewitt. The name."

Ian thought back to his visit to the museum in Barrowford a few weeks ago. The Pendle Witches.

"Hewitt," the policeman repeated, "You think Darren Hewitt was a witch like Katherine Hewitt?"

"Yes!" shouted Liam in triumph, "Yes, Darren is a descendent of Katherine. I've researched his ancestry at the library. He has witchcraft in his blood and I saw the signs."

"Signs?" asked DS Rasheed, thinking that the man before him was rapidly revealing himself to be as mad as a box of frogs.

"Yes! Did you not see the devil sign on his shirt, the satanic pictures on his walls? He was a witch, no doubt in my mind.
Like the Grey woman and Preston and that Charlotte Redferne. All witches. They need to be wiped off the face of the earth. The bible says it. 'Thou shalt not suffer a witch to live,' Exodus. It is God's will"
'Cheryl Hargraves I was not sure. She had the name. Then she came to my flat, offering herself like some Jezebel," his lip curled in disgust, "Then," he jabbed a finger, "Then, I knew. The devil was in her too."

DI Johnson was struggling to maintain a calm composure. Cheryl Hargraves was just lonely, Charlotte Redferne was a young wife and mother, Greta Grey worked defending others and Sarah Preston. Sarah was one of their own. All dead.

"Mr. Horvat," said the DI, in measured tones, "I'm going to stop the interview now, as I need to have a chat with my colleagues. Tape paused at… 1.40am."

DI Johnson paused the tape and left the room with DS Rasheed. They walked swiftly to a room out of earshot.

"Bloody bastard!" spat Ian, "He killed them all!"

DS Rasheed shook his head. He'd heard some things in his time but this was a new one, "I'll get the on-call doctor to assess him. This one's got to be diminished responsibility, don't you think?"

"Yeah, it's looking that way," Ian conceded, "Poor Sarah. It's such a fucking waste. We need to get a Croatian to English interpreter, a psych, and a solicitor for him asap. He might be saying now he doesn't want one, but he's going to need one. We need every I dotted and T crossed on this one or his defense will have a field day"

Chapter FiftyNine. Cheryl.

After speaking to him initially, DI Johnson had already applied for a search warrant for the Liam's ground floor flat. Since then, Liam had also told them about Cheryl.

They waited for daylight. A weak, pale sun dragged itself over the horizon, temporarily filling the sky with warm, oranges and golds that soon faded through lemon and then creams, until all trace of warmth was gone and the sky was colourless. Then, the exhausted sun hung low, lacking strength to rise any higher in the wintry sky. Those involved, wore hazmat suits and had been briefed on what they might find.

Entering the flat, with a key that Liam had said they should use, they immediately felt the cold, and smelled the damp, rotten smell. The curtains and blinds had remained closed. Thin shafts of light that crept in through gaps at the edges of curtains, revealed a myriad dancing dust particles in their beam. The overall feel was gloom and cold and squalor.

The kitchen was full of empty food tins, half a stale loaf and little else. Looking around the darkened flat, they saw the tape around one of the bedroom doors. After photographing it from different angles, and dusting the handle for prints, a sharp Stanley knife was used to slit the tape at the door edges. This meant that any latent fingerprints would be largely undisturbed.

SOCO Jones was assigned to open the door. He took a deep breath before turning the handle and opening it for the first time since the night Cheryl Hargraves had called round with the shepherd's pie.

There was a skittering sound as tiny feet with tiny claws, scampered into the darkness under the bed. Scritch, scratch, scritch as the rats hid, shy of humans.

As his eyes accustomed to the gloom, Jones stepped into the room. There was a strange crunching sound underfoot and pointing his torch to the floor, he saw thousands of dessicated, bluebottle carcasses.

Then, turning the torchbeam toward the bed, he saw the black plastic covered shape which, he had no doubt, was the body of Cheryl Hargraves.

Bodily fluids had seeped through the thin mattress leaving a sticky, stinking, soup on the floor underneath, despite the black plastic. It had dried to a brown tarry mess that would take some effort to remove with paint scrapers.

They decided to move Cheryl, as she was, wrapped up in the bin bags to preserve as much evidence as possible. The cameras flashed numerous times preserving the macabre tableaux for posterity, before Cheryl was packaged in a zip up body bag and carried to the wheeled trolley that would transport her the short way to the waiting vehicle.

When Cheryl was safely on her way to the mortuary, the SOCO's returned to the flat to gather more evidence. A PC stood guard on the door as they worked, protecting the scene from inquisitive folk who watched the enfolding drama with a curious excitement and hoping for some grisly detail to share with their friends.

The white suited officers inside bagged up anything that might be relevant to the case, including Liam's little bible.

It wasn't long before the press arrived, with their cameras and fluffy microphones. Unable to get any comment from the policemen, they went to the neighbours. They asked about Liam, his character and his demeaner, in fact any small detail about him. Had the neighbours seen or suspected anything, or even had they smelled anything? For five minutes of fame, there were a number of more than willing interviewees.

The sun was beginning to dip in the sky by the time police left the site. The reporters were cold and bored, but would have to wait for an official police statement before they could give their viewers any real story, and that wouldn't hapoen until the morning. They packed up their equipment, booked into their hotels for the night then went to warm up in the bar with a few, purely medicinal, drinks.

Chapter Sixty. Farewell.

Sargent John Carpenter was first assigned as Family Liason to Sarah Preston's family, then, after listening to their wishes over cups of tea, John was reassigned as Funeral Coordination Officer for the family. At the request of the family, Sargent Carpenter, had ordered a constabulary flag from the Staff Office. Floral tributes from both the Office of the Police and Crime Commissioner and from Lancashire Constabulary were ordered to be delivered to the chapel of rest where Sarah's body lay. Sargent Carpenter also contacted the Police Federation in regard to financial assistance for Sarah's family.

The family were grateful of John's suggestion of a guard of honour made up of Sarah's colleagues and he made sure letters were sent to those involved informing them of the correct dress, which would be their white shirt and tie uniform with the addition of white gloves and times of pre-funeral rehearsal.

On the day of the funeral, a watery sun rose on a crisp, November morning, shedding a bright, but barely warm, light over the frosty ground. Warm enough however, to evaporate the frozen dew into a mist, that moved languidly, low to the ground, and inbetween the young saplings.

In this unlikely setting, the guard of honour welcomed the body of PC Sarah Preston on her final journey, a salute given by DI Ian Johnson as most senior officer present.

Formal wreaths of white chrysanthemums from the force flanked the grave site and a spray of pretty alstroemeria sat on the constabulary flag that covered the wicker coffin.

The pallbearers laid the coffin gently and reverently on the timber rests and the pagan celebrant began to speak.

"Welcome, to this, a celebration of the life of Sarah Preston, here, at the Woodland Burial Ground at Clitheroe.

I call to the Air in the East, Fire in the South, the Water in the West and Earth in the North. We give you thanks for your provision in our lives.

I ask Meghan, Sarah's sister, to come forward and read Sarah's poem."

Meghan took a deep breath and bravely read a poem her sister had written some time before her death.

" Sarah's Poem, Eternal.

Don't look for me in these dead bones,
I'm gone, my soul flies yonder,
But you will see me, hear me, feel me,
Not as flesh, but something stronger.
In the sun that warms your face,
In the cooling streams of water,
In the earth, that sprouts forth life,
In the wind I whisper.
I am with you, all around you,
I could never flee,

Nor would I want to be without you,
Look to nature, there I'll be.
In the sweetness of the honey,
In each refreshing drop of rain,
In the clouds atop the mountains,
In the goodness of the grain.
I am one with all around,
My energy will never fade,
But be transformed whilst in the ground,
And fill with life this woodland glade."

Meghan finished and returned to her place.
The celebrant then called on DI Johnson to read the eulogy.
He spoke with a great respect for his young colleague, who served the community of Burnley with integrity and diligence. He talked of her dedication to the job and the love her fellow colleagues felt for her.

As DI Johnson returned to his place, the celebrant then signalled for the flowers and the flag to be removed and the haunting voice of Annie Lennox sang out from a small sound system, 'Into the West,' as Sarah was laid to rest.
Finally, one Alstroemeria was given to each person who attended as a momento of Sarah's life that they could press and keep.

Chapter SixtyOne.
Memorium.

Cheryl's sister, Susan, had wanted Cheryl cremated and her ashes brought to Lincolnshire as there were no remaining family in the Burnley area. She had organised Poppets ashes to be sent down also, and she buried the two sets of remains in a beautiful, secluded area of her large garden, marking the site by planting a hardy chrysanthemum called 'Cheryl Pink.' Flowering in the autumn, around the time Cheryl died, and in her favourite lavender pink colour, the chrysanthemum made a fitting memorial. Susan and her husband also bought a white, lutyens style bench and placed it nearby, as a place to sit quietly and remember her.

At the warehouse, Cheryl's workmates, also used the money collected in the jar that had stood, on top of the filing cabinet, in her office to buy a bench for the smoking area. Painted a pastel pink, it was simply inscribed with the words, 'Cheryl's Bench.' on a brass plaque.

Chapter SixtyTwo. Healing.

The art studio was spacious and numerous skylights in the high ceiling flooded the room with natural light. At the moment though, the blinds were drawn so that the screen was clear to see.
Begun as a way of hitting the wellbeing target for the college, the 'Art as Therapy' class was a popular one. Standing at the front of the room, Eve was pointing at the whiteboard screen as she addressed her twelve students.
"So, with chiaroscuro, we're looking at a real, definitive contrast between the light and the shade, the yin and the yang if you like. It gives us quite a harsh, dramatic effect, " Eve spoke to the class. She changed the picture on the screen,

"So here, Carravaggio has used this technique to great effect. The body, here, appears almost luminescent against the darkness of the surroundings. It makes the body stand out. He is in the definite fore compared to the receding dark. It's giving depth to the painting. Light colours look closer, dark colours recede. See how 'real' it looks, it's not flat.

Look at the body. He almost glows. It's saying, 'Here is this man, pure, good, light, but he exists in darkness, in a world that is his opposite.' Carravaggio is emphasising and exaggerating the difference to make his point.

Ok any questions before we have a go? "

A young woman in her mid twenties, began to speak,

" So it's like the dark is symbolic of evil? " she asked hesitantly.

" Yes, Chloe. I think so. Carravaggio isn't here for us to ask, but yes. Jesus was called, 'The light of the world' in the bible, it tells Christians to, 'be the light,' and also the concept of being spiritually blind really keys in to the ideas of something pure, light and good in an inherently dark and evil world."

Chloe nodded and began to draw.

Eve pulled the cords that opened the blinds, and the studio filled with light.

" I'm going to leave the picture on the screen, but of course, you can choose any subject matter, it's using the chiaroscuro technique that I'm looking for, the subject is secondary," Eve finished and then sat down to complete the online register.

The room fell silent as the students focused on their charcoal drawings. Eve played some quiet, calming music on the computer as background to their work.

Chloe became totally involved in her drawing. She drew a swan, on a lake, with it's wings outstretched, as though it was about to take flight, but the dark water formed a hand that had hold of the swan's feet, dragging it down. She drew dark thunderous clouds. The white swan surrounded by darkness.

Eve began to slowly walk around the class, looking over the students work. She stopped at Chloe's table.

"That's excellent Chloe. I like the contrast you've made between the white swan and the dark water," commented Eve.

"The swan is an innocent," explained Chloe, being dragged down by the world, never able to soar. "

Nodding, Eve saw the sadness in the drawing. She had heard that Chloe had lost her sister last year, and saw her raw pain in each stroke of charcoal. Seeing the class as a way to work through some of the difficult emotions she was experiencing, Chloe had joined as a kind of therapy following Courtney's death. She was getting there, gradually. Bereavement was a process. She still had days where she didn't even want to get out of bed, but now, she could at least see light at the end of the tunnel. Her fiancé was a fantastic support as was her mum. The class was a way of getting all the 'stuff' she carried around, out, to be dealt with.

Eve meandered through the room, stopping to give critique or suggestions as she went.

Towards the end of the class, Eve invited everyone to share their work and explain the thought processes behind it. They were such a supportive group, listening intently and praising the raw honesty of each students contribution, whether technically good or not. Sometimes there were tears, but this was a safe place to share and Eve felt privileged to be a small part of their healing.

Eve was packing up the sticks of charcoal as the students left for home. Chloe hung back wanting to speak privately with Eve.

Eve looked up and smiled at Chloe, "Did you want me for something?"

Chloe nodded and walked up to Eve.

"I just wanted to thank you," began Chloe, "This class is really helping me. Every week, when I leave, I feel a little bit lighter. I didn't think just drawing or painting would make a difference, but it does! I'm not sure why or how, but it is helping, and I'm even enjoying it! "

Eve smiled, "I'm really happy to hear that Chloe. Any outlet for our emotions can help; painting, poetry, writing, music. All can help. Am so pleased to hear you're enjoying the course. It makes it all worthwhile."

They walked out of the studio together, talking about art and emotions. They said their goodbyes at the carpark and Eve climbed into her little, silver mini with a smile, feeling she had actually had a positive impact on real lives through her work. She couldn't wait to get home and let her husband, Ian, know how well Chloe was doing. Ian Johnson was a detective inspector. He knew, because of his last murder case which involved the sexual exploitation of minors, that the whole family had been through so much and a bit of positive news would do him good.

Chapter SixtyThree. Madness.

Liam read from his Croatian Bible as he read every night and every morning. He was chosen to suffer for Christ. That's what Liam believed in the very core of his being. He had been chosen. He could feel it. In his mind, in his heart, in every pore of his skin, in the pit of his stomach, in his balls, everywhere, he knew, with no shadow of doubt.
He. Was. Chosen.
He thanked God for the privilege of suffering in the name of Jesus. Liam avowed to serve well, with all of his strength.
That's what he told the Psychiatrist who spent time assessing his state of mind. Dr. Sebastian Black listened patiently and wrote notes in a hardbacked notenook.
'childhood trauma, hyperreligiosity, social difficulties, delusional thinking, self mortification, mania
Possible schizophrenia?
bi-polar psychosis?'

Liam kept talking. He explained that by following the geneologies, he had tracked down descendents of the Pendle witches. He'd then investigated these descendents for any signs of them practising witchcraft using social media, google searches and even following them around town. He knew Greta Grey was a member of a witchcraft Facebook group, Charlotte Redferne practised necromancy and divination in her Facebook live chats, even making a lucrative living from hoodwinking the gullible. Sarah Preston, he discovered, was a member of a local coven of witches that met regularly in the modern equivalent of their Malkin Tower and Darren Hewitt wore pagan symbols and listened to music that Liam considered demonic. All evidence, in Liam's delusional thinking, that led to their death sentence.

As for Cheryl, she had the witch gene, but she was also a sinful, wanton Jezebel. She'd tried to seduce him, enchant him. He had to kill her. Then he had to get rid of the car. He told the Psychiatrist how.

He'd stangled her. It took some time. She put up a good fight, but in the end he managed it.

Then he sat for a while, in shock he supposed. He hadn't planned to kill her.

It was two in the morning. He adjusted the drivers seat of the Renault clio to suit his longer legs. He turned the ignition and started the engine.

Driving away in the little car, he wondered what to do with it. Dump it on the moors? Set it in fire? Where was it Cheryl lived? He'd seen the outside of her house once, when they'd shared a cab after a works do. She'd invited him in for coffee which he respectfully declined and continued the journey to his own home.

Spotting the house after driving slowly down Cheryl's street, he turned into the driveway and parked the little car. Sitting inside, he got Cheryl's mobile phone out of his pocket. Luckily, Cheryl had no complicated code to open it and he typed out a text message to work,

'Sorry, but I won't be in work this week. I have a bad ear infection and the doctor has told me to stay at home and rest.'

Getting out of the car, he threw the keys into the laurel bushes and quickly walked away.

Around a week later, he couldn't remember an exact date but it was after his mother's funeral, he arrived home.

Turning his key in the lock, Liam immediately noticed the smell. It hadn't seemed too bad this morning, but time away had reawakened his nose to the pungent odour. It pervaded the whole place.

It was Cheryl. He'd put her on his mother's bed as he wasn't sure what else to do with her. Now though, it was becoming a problem. Liam sat down to think. The neighbours might start to ask questions or worse, phone someone to come and investigate the source of the terrible stench.

There were two options.

He needed to either move her or seal in the smell somehow. He couldn't take her on the back of his bike and had no other transport. Sealing her in seemed the only viable option.

Retrieving his old, metal, tool box from the tall cupboard that housed the vacuum cleaner and various other useful items, he searched through its trays full of screwdrivers, alun keys and drill bits, until he found the duct tape. Just the job, he thought to himself. He also got out binliners, his mother's yellow rubber gloves and an old tub of shake n vac that had been under the sink for years.

Steeling himself, he opened the door to his mother's room. The stench of putrefaction hit him like a warm wall of invisible, miasmic fog. Coughing, his nose wrinkled and he felt a repugnance he'd never felt before.

There she lay.

Cheryl.

Though he could barely recognise her now. In life, he'd found Cheryl and her clumsy sexual advances repulsive. In death, he found her utterly abhorrent.

Despite him keeping all the heating turned off, her skin had begun to turn black in places, a greenish tinge in others. Its surface was shiny and tight under pressure from liquifying cells. Her dyed auburn hair still looked as it did in life, though now it had a somewhat wiglike appearance due to the contrast with the disfigured face. Her eyes were yellowed and protruding giving her a strange, startled expression and around her open mouth, the vivid pink lipstick now looked hideously obscene and he began to gag.

Liam took a black bin liner and slid it over Cheryl's head, and another over her lower body. As he lifted her leg, the skin broke and slipped under his gloved hand, sliding free from the flesh beneath. Dropping the leg in surprise and revulsion, he felt the acidic burn and bitter taste of bile rise in his throat. Regaining his composure, he lifted the legs a second time and slid the black binliner up around them. Fluids leaking from Cheryl as tissues broke down, had left dark staining on the bare mattress in a macabre outline of her corpse.

He taped both bags tight to Cheryl's body. This left just the middle section. First he sprinkled the shake n vac powder over the mattress and over Cheryl's midsection. The synthetic floral scent barely made a difference to the stink. Liam taped one bag to another, laying them over her tummy and tucking them under her bottom. Pulling out more lengths of tape, he attached the middle bags to those on her head and legs.

Standing back and looking at his handiwork, he decided that it wasn't perfect but it was going to have to do.

Next, he taped all around the windows, sealing them shut, then the ventilation brick and finally, he closed the door and sealed around the edges with the tape. The door to his mother's room would remain sealed permanently from now on.

After bagging up the gloves and the empty shake n vac and putting them in the bin outside, he opened wide all the windows in the other rooms in an attempt to clear the air.

Leaving them open, Liam ran himself a bath and climbed in for a soak, trying to rid himself of any lingering trace of Cheryl. He lay there, unsuccessfully trying to stop his mind racing and relax.

Then he just forgot about her, he told Doctor Sebastian with a shrug of his shoulders.

His psychiatrist would recommend a course of treatment, including anti psychotic medication together with talking therapies and a defence of 'diminished responsibility' to a murder charge.

Darren recovered well. So well in fact, that six months later, he asked Janet and her two children to move in with him, and Janet agreed. She soon, as women are apt to do, began making changes to the house. Little feminine touches which Darren took in his stride, welcoming the extra cushions on the sofa, the softer colours on the walls and even the noise and clutter of small children.

Darren and Janet were content. They loved each other and both loved the children and that, my friend, is one of life's rarest gifts. If you find love, value it and treasure it. Hate steals joy. Love expands to fill any space.

Chapter SixtyFour. Blessed.

A precarious peace had descended on Burnley. People were still a little nervous, if the unthinkable had happened once, it could happen again right?

Parents kept a closer eye on their children and hugged them a little tighter goodnight. Husbands ran their wives home from work rather than let them catch the bus or walk in the dark.

Thankfully, the killer had been caught and removed from their community.

Was Liam himself a victim? Driven mad by war, fear and loss? Maybe, but that didn't heal the grief of the children he left motherless, or the parents he left bereft, or the husband heartbroken. It didn't bring back Greta, Charlotte, Sarah or Cheryl. We don't demand an eye for an eye, but we do demand protection and atonement, so Liam, though not deemed fit to stand trial, is destined for life in an institution for the criminally insane.

In another week or so, festive Christmas decorations would shine in place of those for Halloween. Lights in the darkness, adding a cheery glow to the streets of Burnley and bringing laughter and merriment, peace and goodwill, but most of all, hope.

As for today, the wintery sun had dipped below the horizon and the bluey purples of evening coloured the Lancashire sky. The ground was hard and unforgiving and the black skeletal trees had shed the last of their fire coloured leaves.

Ian was on a weeks leave now the case was closed, and the Johnson household had just finished dinner. Ian was washing up the pasta bowl and plates. Joel was upstairs in his room playing some kind of shooting game on his Ps4 and Eve sat in one of the wicker chairs that faced out of the french doors, looking over the garden. She was sipping her glass of chilled pouilly fumé, feeling full and perfectly relaxed.

Looking through the glass at the autumn garden with its scattered lights like miniature moons she suddenly saw him in the undergrowth.

She froze. Hardly daring to breathe. It couldn't be. Her eyes grew wide as she stared out into the darkness. Had Ian seen?

Keeping her eyes fixed on him, watching for any movement, she stayed perfectly still.

She didn't know how to attract her husband's attention without breaking the spell. Catching Ian in her peripheral vision, she saw he was standing perfectly still too, gazing out, spellbound.

He stepped cautiously out of the undergrowth and onto the lawn.

In their garden, lit softly by the moon, stood a majestic stag. Resplendent in his winter coat, thick and full, made mercurial by the silver light. His antlers held proudly aloft, still covered in their soft velvet.

Rose had once said that seeing a deer was a good omen. As a spirit animal, it symbolised peace, kindness and serenity.

The stag dipped his magnificent head to the ground and began to eat one of the last of the windfall apples that lay on the lawn. Eve was enchanted by the beautiful animal. She risked a glance at Ian, who looked back as excited as she was at the rare sight. They stared at the magical creature, both feeling blessed to have seen him. After perhaps a minute, maybe two, the deer startled, and in an instant was gone.

"Oh my goodness!" said Eve breathlessly, "He was beautiful!"

"I know!" said Ian incredulously, "Wow!"

Ian poured himself a glass of the pouilly fumé and came to sit in the second wicker chair, opposite his wife.

"That was amazing!" he said, still excited, "I'd heard that there were red deer on the hills but I've never seen one."

"He was absolutely breath taking," agreed Eve, "We are so incredibly lucky you know."

She took hold of Ian's hand and felt so overwhelmed that tears began to prick at her eyes. Ian softly kissed her hand, "We are very lucky."